O9-AIC-987

They had agreed not to see each other again, then she shows up out of the blue on his doorstep?

Then he realized he was nervous.

Nervous and excited to see her, even though he knew any relationship between them would lead to a dead end.

The attraction, the soul-deep connection that he'd tried to write off as a fluke, was apparently no fluke after all. His first instinct was to tug her into his arms and kiss her senseless.

"This is awkward, huh?"

"Yeah. I seem to recall that we agreed not to see each other again."

"I know," she said. "And I'm sorry, but the situation has changed."

He folded his arms across his chest and leaned back. "Which situation is that?"

She took a deep breath and blew it out, then looked him in the eye and said, "The situation that arose when I found out I was pregnant."

Dear Reader,

As a mother of three, I have always loved pregnancy stories. There is no time in a couple's life more exciting, frightening or rewarding.

Or confusing.

Like most expectant parents, Miranda and Zack experience all of the above. To complicate matters, they possess two completely opposing sets of values and conflicting careers. They also have chemistry, physical and emotional, so getting these two together was a breeze. Keeping them together, on the other hand, was the hard part. They constantly had me wondering how two intelligent, educated adults could act so...*dumb*. They're so busy trying to live by the standards they set, they forget to *live*.

In the end they must decide if they want to live the life they've chosen, or choose the life they want. I hope you enjoy their journey as much as I did.

Michelle Celmer

ACCIDENTALLY EXPECTING

MICHELLE CELMER

Silhouette

SPECIAL EDITION

Published by Silhouette Books

America's Publisher of Contemporary Romance

If you purchased this book without a cover you should be aware
that this book is stolen property. It was reported as "unsold and
destroyed" to the publisher, and neither the author nor the
publisher has received any payment for this "stripped book."

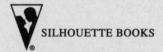

SILHOUETTE BOOKS

ISBN-13: 978-0-373-24847-6
ISBN-10:   0-373-24847-4

ACCIDENTALLY EXPECTING

Copyright © 2007 by Michelle Celmer

All rights reserved. Except for use in any review, the reproduction
or utilization of this work in whole or in part in any form by any
electronic, mechanical or other means, now known or hereafter
invented, including xerography, photocopying and recording, or in
any information storage or retrieval system, is forbidden without
the written permission of the editorial office, Silhouette Books,
233 Broadway, New York, NY 10279 U.S.A.

This is a work of fiction. Names, characters, places and incidents are
either the product of the author's imagination or are used fictitiously, and
any resemblance to actual persons, living or dead, business establishments,
events or locales is entirely coincidental.

This edition published by arrangement with Harlequin Books S.A.

® and TM are trademarks of Harlequin Books S.A., used under license.
Trademarks indicated with ® are registered in the United States Patent
and Trademark Office, the Canadian Trade Marks Office and in other
countries.

Visit Silhouette Books at www.eHarlequin.com

Printed in U.S.A.

Books by Michelle Celmer

Silhouette Special Edition

Accidentally Expecting #1847

Silhouette Desire

Playing by the Baby Rules #1566
The Seduction Request #1626
Bedroom Secrets #1656
Round-the-Clock Temptation #1683
House Calls #1703
The Millionaire's Pregnant Mistress #1739
The Secretary's Secret #1774
Best Man's Conquest #1799

Silhouette Romantic Suspense

Running on Empty #1342
Out of Sight #1398

MICHELLE CELMER

lives in a southeastern Michigan zoo.

Well, okay, it's really a house, but with three teenagers, three dogs, three cats (are you seeing a pattern here?) and a fifty-gallon tank full of various marine life, sometimes it feels like a zoo. It's rarely quiet, seldom clean, and between after-school jobs, various extracurricular activities and band practice, getting everyone home at the same time to share a meal is next to impossible.

To Courtney
You may be my niece,
but in my heart you'll always be my sister

Chapter One

Married to a bully? Have you had enough? Emotional abuse leaves no bruises, breaks no bones, still the damage runs deep. Think it's impossible to prove? Think again. A tape recorder or hidden camera can be a girl's best friend.

—excerpt from *The Modern Woman's Guide to Divorce (and the joys of staying single)*

She was going to seduce him.

Miranda Reed sat in the shadows at the back of the hotel lounge, sipping her apple martini, eyes on her prey. He sat alone at the bar, his attention on the football game, unaware that he was being watched. His suit jacket lay draped on the bar stool beside him, and he'd rolled the sleeves of his shirt and loosened his tie. Even in this casual, relaxed state he stood out from the other businessmen. Everything about him was slightly and subtly exaggerated.

At six-two, Zackary Jameson stood a hair taller than most men, with a physique toned to perfection, dressed in a suit and shirt that were obviously tailor-made to accentuate every one of his assets. She was especially impressed by the "asset" resting on the bar stool.

She did so appreciate a man with a nice rear end.

He somehow managed a perpetual tan, without ever looking leathery or sun baked, and any signs of age on his face made him look more distinguished than old. His short dark hair had that sexy, mussed look, as if he'd just run his hands through it wet, but in reality probably took hours in front of a mirror to perfect. His mouth was wide, his smile warm and genuine, and his teeth just white and straight enough. Caps, she was guessing. No one had teeth that perfect naturally.

He carried himself with casual authority, an ease and male grace that made people stop and watch.

She'd never met a man who radiated such confidence, who was more comfortable in his own skin.

Too bad he was an overopinionated male chauvinist pig whose ideologies fell out of fashion with covered wagons and hoop skirts.

When asked to do the radio show with the renowned relationship guru, a man who had built an empire around the principles of traditional family values, her publicist assured her the promotion for the book she cowrote, *The Modern Woman's Guide to Divorce (and the joys of staying single),* would be invaluable.

Big mistake.

He'd argued so logically and twisted her words so skillfully that by the end of the show her message had been lost and she'd come out looking like a radical feminist man hater.

She couldn't forget the way he'd watched her with those piercing blue eyes, eyes deep enough to swim in, with not a hint of the superiority and satisfaction he must have been feeling for discrediting her. In fact, as she'd become angrier and more aggressive, he'd stayed calm and reasonable, the drivel he preached pouring out of him, smothering her every point like hot fudge over cold vanilla ice cream.

Call it petty and uncivilized, but she was in the

mood for some good old-fashioned revenge. Even if she would be the only one who knew.

She was going to put his high ideals to the test and see if he really believed all that garbage he spouted about marriage and family. Specifically, his views on intimacy. The slightly updated version of no sex before marriage. The idea that a man and a woman should be committed, preferably with plans of marriage, before consummating a relationship.

They would just see about that.

Miranda watched as the waitress delivered the drink she had ordered him, saw the look of curiosity on his face. The waitress pointed in her direction, and when he turned, she pasted on an alluring smile and waggled her fingers at him. One of those heart-stopping grins curled the corners of his mouth when he recognized her.

He tossed a few bills on the waitress's tray—a man like him would of course be a generous tipper—grabbed his jacket and drink and headed to her table, his eyes never leaving her face. She'd worn her hair down and let it fall in silky waves over her shoulders, its dark color bringing out the green in her eyes. It was a little unnerving the way he stared with such intensity, as if the world around them no longer existed. As he drew closer she even felt a little breathless, as if he'd sucked all the air from the room and there was none left for her.

This night could definitely prove to be satisfying, in more ways than one.

"Mr. Jameson," she said as he stopped beside the table.

"Ms. Reed," he replied, with an affable tip of his head. He had the voice of a radio DJ—deep and mesmerizing. A voice that held captive auditoriums full of his loyal supporters for hours on end. "May I join you?"

She gestured to the empty seat, taking care to make the move look as gracefully seductive as possible. If there was one thing she'd learned on her journey to becoming a modern, independent woman, it was how to seduce a man. "Please."

He set his drink on the table and hung his jacket on the back of the chair before he slid into the seat, casual yet so controlled, as if he thoroughly planned each and every move before executing it. "Are you enjoying your stay in New York?"

"It's been...*interesting.*" Not to mention frustrating and humiliating. "Between the book signings and the interviews it's been an exhausting couple of days. I'm looking forward to getting back to Dallas."

"I had hoped to have time to speak with you after the broadcast."

"So you could rub the victory in my face maybe?" she asked, keeping her tone sweet.

He smiled. "No, so I could tell you what a pleasure it was to meet you. I enjoyed our discussion. I was impressed."

She shot him a disbelieving look. "Could have fooled me."

He just smiled. "Do you still practice law?"

"Not recently, no. The book seems to have dominated my life."

"I take you're not a litigator."

"Gee, what tipped you off?"

He relaxed back in his seat and sipped his drink, studying her for a long moment. "I could tell you exactly what you did wrong during that interview. How you lost control."

She folded her arms and leaned forward, resting them on the table, giving him a nice view of her cleavage, thanks to her very-low-cut, scoop neck silk blouse. "This should be good."

His eyes didn't stray from her face. "You attacked me. You spent all of your time trying to convince me that your way is better. That your opinions hold more credibility."

"Isn't that exactly what *you* do?"

"Quite the opposite. I never once said that what you believe is wrong."

She opened her mouth to argue, then paused, trying to remember a single thing he'd said to debunk her. But damned if he wasn't right. Not once had he directly challenged her opinion or disagreed with her. While she'd been quick to accuse him of being old-fashioned and closed-minded he'd simply stated his point of view logically and calmly.

She hadn't *lost* control. She'd never had it.

"It is not my goal or intention to persuade people to live a cardboard-cut-out lifestyle," he said.

She let out a very uncouth, unsexy snort of disbelief. "That is *exactly* your goal."

"I disagree." He was so damned calm and rational. It was as annoying as it was fascinating. "What I do is give people options. A very basic principle of family dynamics. Whether they choose to adopt that lifestyle, or how they integrate it into their own lives, in whole or part, is entirely up to the individual."

As much as she hated admitting she was wrong, and hated *being* wrong even more, in his books, which she'd grudgingly skimmed, and the seminar she'd rented on DVD, she couldn't recall a single incident when he'd said his way was the only way. Maybe that was what made people so receptive to his ideas.

She tried a different angle. "You're not married. In fact, I read that you've never been married."

"Not yet," he agreed.

"Why not?"

He shrugged. "I guess I just haven't met the right woman."

"Maybe that's because the kind of woman you're looking for doesn't exist."

"I don't believe that. Everyone has a soul mate. I just haven't met mine yet."

"Considering your views on sex before marriage, you must lead a very…*lonely* existence."

"I believe in waiting until the relationship becomes exclusive and committed before sex. And though I've never been married, I've been in several committed relationships." He leaned forward slightly, flashing her a playful, sexy look that had her toes curling in her spiked heels. "Very *satisfying* committed relationships."

Oh, boy, who was doing the seducing here? Or maybe he was just a tease. Either way, she was having far too much fun. And he had no idea who he was messing with. Considering his conservative views on relationships, she could only assume he would be equally conservative in the bedroom. Given her preference to be in charge, the arrangement would work well for her. Maybe she could teach him a thing or two.

She sipped her drink, looking up at him through

the fringe of her lashes. "How can a man who has never been married be an authority on marriage?"

"Does a psychiatrist have to have schizophrenia to treat it? Does a defense attorney have to be a criminal to represent his client?"

The man had an answer for everything, didn't he? Yet it was fascinating to watch, really, to see the way his mind worked. He was passionate without being arrogant, staunch in his views but not intolerant of her opinions. It also didn't hurt that he was gorgeous, had a body to die for and a more than decent sense of humor.

As they chatted and sipped their drinks, she found herself lulled by his voice, trapped in the depths of his eyes. There were women all around them but he never spared one a single glance. His eyes were on her only. His steady gaze made her feel as if she were the only one in the universe.

More than two hours and several drinks later, despite the fact that she was beginning to feel more than a little tipsy, they were still at it. Still talking and debating. And all she could think about was getting him up to her room, liberating him from his clothing and showing him a thing or two about real women. What would his lips feel like? How would he taste? Would he take charge, or would he lie back and let her be in control?

Her yearning for revenge was overshadowed by a much more basic instinct. Good old-fashioned sexual attraction. She and Zack may have had completely opposite views on relationships, but they also had chemistry. A lethal combination of hormones, pheromones and testosterone.

She could tell that he felt it, too. The longer they sat there, the more aware of each other they became. Aware and distracted. His eyes began to stray to her cleavage, their gaze as intimate and exciting as a caress, but pure somehow. He watched her mouth as she sipped her drink, making every move feel slow and exaggerated. Seductive and sexy. When his foot bumped hers under the table, she didn't doubt the move was intentional. Instead of feeling violated, she wanted to be closer. She became aware of herself leaning in toward him and saw that he was doing the same. As if they both felt compelled to be closer. The pull of attraction was irresistible.

Had it not been for the table between them and the fact that they were in public, she didn't doubt that they would be wrapped around each other by now.

She looked around and realized the bar had nearly emptied. Zack looked at his watch. "It's late."

"Up past your bedtime?" she asked, attempting

to keep a teasing tone, so he wouldn't see her disappointment. Had she misread his signals? Was he not as turned on as she was? Or did he really stick by the no-sex rule?

"I was thinking maybe it was past yours. Could I walk you to your room?" He flashed her another one of those sexy smiles, gave her a look that said he wanted to do a lot more than just walk her to her room, and she felt a zing of excitement from her scalp down to the tips of her toes and some very interesting places in between.

She had him right where she wanted him.

Or did he have her?

"I had a good time tonight," Miranda told Zack as they stepped off the elevator onto her floor. When they'd been standing side by side, she'd been even more aware of his size, his imposing presence. She'd always considered herself average in height, but in three-inch heels she was still a good five or six inches shorter than him.

The grace of his movements, the sheer masculinity, was hypnotizing. This was a man who looked good and he knew it. Yet he managed not to come off as arrogant.

How did he do that?

Her hands itched to touch him, to unfasten the

buttons of his shirt and explore the skin underneath. But she had to play this just right. She had to be subtle. He'd been a perfect gentleman in the lobby and while they rode up the twenty-two floors alone in the elevator. The only physical contact he'd made was to gently touch her elbow. Not that she'd expected him to ravage her in public.

Not that it wouldn't have been exciting to know he was so taken he couldn't resist her.

"I had a good time, too," he said, flashing her a grin. "It's refreshing to have a discussion with someone who doesn't agree with everything I say."

"You're different than I expected."

"What did you expect?"

"Truthfully? I expected you to be an arrogant male-chauvinist pig."

He didn't look offended. In fact, his smile widened. "You wouldn't be the first person to accuse me of that. I understand that my philosophies can be tough to swallow for some people."

"If it's any consolation, I may not agree with your ideas, but I do respect them. It would be great if life really worked that way. Unfortunately, I know better."

They reached her room and she dug in her purse for the key card, but her fingers didn't seem to be working as well as usual. When she found it, he plucked it from her fingers and unlocked the door. He held it open and she stepped into her room, turning to him with every intention of inviting him in. Before she could get a word out, he'd backed her inside, shut the door and pulled her into his arms.

Chapter Two

Pressed up against the long, warm, solid length of Zack's body, Miranda had no doubt of his attraction for her. The man was definitely turned on, and he was apparently big all over.

A lamp beside the bed shed soft light in the room and she could see the desire in his eyes. Her first instinct was to resist, to push him away. He had stepped in and taken control of a situation she'd intended to direct and she felt the tiniest bit apprehensive. But her body wouldn't listen to her head. She didn't know if it was the drinks making her fuzzy or the two hours of verbal foreplay blurring her good sense, but she trembled all over. She caught the hint of a subtle and clean-scented after-shave mixed with some familiar brand of soap, neither of which covered his own unique masculine scent.

She hadn't expected this. She was the one who was supposed to be seducing him. She had to do something to win back the control.

"All I've been able to think about tonight was touching you," he rasped, caressing her face. The move was gentle and firm at the same time. Then he kissed her—deep, intense and disarming—and she went limp with desire. He was a man on a mission. He knew what he wanted and wasn't shy about taking it.

How could something so wrong feel so good? When it came to sex she was always the aggressor; she called the shots. This all seemed to be moving too fast, yet she didn't make a move to stop him.

She didn't want to stop him.

He kissed her mouth, her throat, tasting and nipping her skin, as if he wanted to devour every inch of her. He bit her earlobe hard enough to make her gasp with surprise and her body shudder in ecstasy.

He shrugged out of his jacket and tossed it aside, but when she tried to unbutton his shirt he manacled her wrists and held them behind her, backing her against the door. A move like that would earn any other man a swift knee jerk to the crotch, but no other man had ever made her feel so willing to let go.

He trapped both of her wrists in one large hand and used the other to unfasten the buttons on her blouse. She probably could have broken loose, but at this point she didn't want to be free.

He pushed her blouse off her shoulders. It slipped down her arms and caught on her wrists. She wasn't exactly large-busted, but her breasts sat firm and high and were nicely shaped. With the exception of her ex-husband, who found fault with everything, she'd never heard a single complaint.

Considering the way Zack was looking at her, he wouldn't be complaining, either. His assessing eyes burned her skin like hot coals. She'd worked damned hard for this body. She knew she looked good and he appeared to agree.

He lowered his head, biting her though the lacy fabric of her bra, blowing hot breath on her skin. She moaned and arched her back.

"I don't do this," he said, looking at her with an intensity that gave her chills. "I don't have affairs with women I just met and hardly even know."

"I don't, either," she admitted.

"I've never wanted a woman the way I want you right now."

Zack's words filled her with a thrilling kind of satisfaction. But for all the wrong reasons. Reasons that had nothing to do with revenge. This was all about wanting Zack. Wanting him to ravage her. She would go so far as to say she needed him, but she didn't *need* anyone.

He cupped the back of her thigh, dragging her skirt up, growling with pleasure when he realized she was wearing a garter belt. Since her divorce from a man who didn't think sexy underwear was "appropriate," she'd spent hundreds of dollars on all the racy things he had never let her wear. It was nice to meet someone who appreciated her taste.

Zack let go of her wrists and her blouse fell to the floor. He unzipped her skirt and smoothed it down her hips, leaving her in only a scandalously brief and sheer bra and thong set, a lace garter belt, black silk stockings and spike heels. She'd never felt so sexy in all her life.

He dropped to his knees in front of her and nuzzled his face against her bare stomach, his beard stubble abrading her skin, making her shiver. Every part of her felt alive with sexual awareness and heavy with lust. He nibbled her stomach, ran his tongue over the tiny gold hoop in her navel, gripping her hips in his big hands.

He tugged roughly on her thong and she heard it rip apart in his hands, but she was too excited to care that he'd ruined her favorite one. He could rip it all if that was what he wanted, if that would excite him even half as much as he'd excited her.

Her body felt shaky and weak, and she tunneled her fingers though his hair to hold herself steady. Her breath was coming faster, her anticipation mounting, and when he finally buried his face between her thighs she cried out. Her body arched, fingers tangled in his hair. Her knees gave out, but he caught her before she could fall and hooked her leg over his shoulder. She was on the verge of a cataclysmic explosion, the sparks sizzling ever closer to the end of her fuse.

When it reached her core, the explosions rocked through her. It was so good, so perfect, she wanted to cry. In her life no one had ever made her feel this way. It scared her half to death and thrilled her beyond belief.

She was too limp to even think twice as he lifted her off her feet and deposited her on the bed. Too sated to do anything but watch as he undressed. His body was just as amazing as she'd thought it would be.

He knelt on the bed beside her and pulled her shoes off one at a time, tossing them to the floor. When she reached up to undo her bra, he stopped her.

"Keep it on." His eyes raking over her as he knelt between her thighs. He hooked his hands around the backs of her knees and tugged her closer, the coarse hair on his legs tickling her skin. His actions were demanding and almost overpowering, yet somehow managed to be tender.

Then he closed his eyes and cursed, a four-letter word she didn't think men like him used.

"What's wrong?"

"I just realized, I don't have protection."

No protection? What man in this day and age didn't carry condoms?

The kind who didn't have sex until he was in a committed relationship, which she was guessing typically took more than two hours and three Scotch on the rocks.

Lucky for him a modern woman was always prepared. She had been anticipating this.

"In my purse."

He reached over and grabbed it for her, and after she dug a condom out, he tried to take it from her.

"Oh, no," she said, ripping it open. "This is my favorite part."

She watched him watching her, the heat in his eyes as she rolled it on. Then she reached up and threaded her fingers behind his neck, pulling him to her, his warm weight sinking her into the mattress without squashing her. Every part of him felt warm and strong and solid.

He kissed her, the deep soul-searching kind, while he tortured her with small thrusts of his hips. She clung to him, sinking her nails into his shoulders, his backside, her body arching with impatience. She'd never felt so out of control, so swept away with lust. It was as if Zack wanted to see her beg for it, wanted her to know she was completely under his control, and she was. She would do anything he wanted right now. Anything he asked.

It frightened her almost as much as it turned her on.

After that, everything became a mystifying blur of intense sensation. Sights and sounds and feelings all jumbled together into something so overpowering she couldn't even name it. And when they reached the peak together, she knew her idea of what sex was supposed to be had been inexplicably changed.

This was what it felt like to really connect with another person. To be separate, but one.

And she could never see Zachary Jameson again.

* * *

Zack sat in his home office at the computer, where he did most of his work these days, attempting to write the syndicated monthly column that was due on the editor's desk by the end of the week. Unfortunately, all he'd been able to think about in the past two months since his trip to New York was Miranda Reed.

He wasn't typically attracted to strong, independent women, and he'd never slept with a woman on the first date. Not since college, anyway. But there was something about her he'd found impossible to resist, something that prompted him to reject his own morals and put his reputation on the line.

A million little things, which all wrapped up together, had him craving her company, her touch.

But they had agreed, despite their attraction, that to pursue any kind of relationship would be a waste of time. Not only did they live a thousand miles from each other, they had conflicting beliefs and values. She wasn't interested in a commitment and he had no desire for a short-term relationship based solely on sex.

What they had was an extreme case of opposites attract. Two people who had nothing in common but good sex.

No, not good sex. *Great* sex. Mind-blowing sex.

And absolutely no future together.

He'd done a fairly decent job of convincing himself they were both better off. But there was still a little voice in the back of his mind asking, what if he'd made a mistake letting her go? Unfortunately, he'd found listening to that little voice to be irrational and ill-advised.

His desk phone rang. Line two, his doorman. He only called up if Zack had a guest, and he wasn't expecting anyone. Nor was he in the mood for company.

He picked up the phone anyway. "Yes, Danny."

"Someone here to see you, Mr. Jameson. A Ms. Reed."

For a second he was sure he misunderstood. "Ms. *who?*"

"Miranda Reed, sir. Shall I send her up?"

What the hell was Miranda doing in Chicago? And why was she here, at his building? How did she even know where he lived?

"Sir?"

He shook off the sudden confusion. "Yeah, sure. Go ahead and send her up."

He hung up the phone and sat there for a second feeling dazed and bewildered. They had agreed not to see each other again, then she shows up out of the blue on his doorstep? What was she up to?

When the doorbell chimed, he rose from his desk

and walked to the front door, the whole situation feeling a bit surreal. Then he realized he was nervous.

Nervous and excited to see her, even though he knew any relationship between them would lead to a dead end. Unless she'd had a drastic change of heart and, as she'd so aptly phrased it, succumbed to the allure of the dark side, there was no reason for her to come here.

He pulled open the door and there she stood, dressed casually in low-slung flared jeans, a denim jacket and a jewel-encrusted T-shirt that rode up just high enough to show off her navel ring. She looked young and sassy and hip, a completely different spin on the no-nonsense alluring woman he'd taken up to her room.

The way she looked him up and down, taking in his faded jeans, T-shirt and bare feet, she was probably thinking the same thing.

The attraction, the soul-deep connection that he'd tried to write off as a fluke, was apparently no fluke after all. His first instinct was to tug her into his arms and kiss her senseless.

It struck him as odd that they'd been so intimate, and they barely knew one another. Yet he felt as though they were connected somehow. He knew her, even though he didn't know her.

"Hi," she finally said.

"Hi."

She shifted nervously. "So, I'll bet you're surprised to see me."

That was an understatement. Did she think she could bounce in and out of his life like a ping-pong ball?

She fidgeted with the bottom edge of her jacket. "I hope it's not a problem. My stopping by unannounced, I mean."

He folded his arms over his chest. "I guess that depends on what you want."

"What I want?" She looked confused, then the meaning of his words seemed to sink in. "Oh, I'm only here to talk."

He couldn't imagine what they had left to talk about. But at the very least, he should listen to what she had to say.

He backed up and gestured her inside.

She stepped past him, taking in the foyer and the living room with curiosity. "The penthouse, huh? Very nice."

"Thanks." They stood there for a moment in awkward silence, so he asked, "Can I take your jacket?"

"No, thanks." She rubbed her arms absently, as if fighting off a chill. "I'm not used to this cool weather. It's a lot hotter in May in Texas."

"Would you care for something warm to drink? Tea? Coffee?"

"Water?"

"Kitchen is this way," he said, and she followed him. "Did you just get into town?"

"I came right from the airport. I apologize for dropping in out of the blue. I would have called first, but the truth is, until I walked into the building, I wasn't sure if I could really do this."

"But here you are."

"Yeah. Here I am."

He filled a glass with filtered water and handed it to her. She barely took a sip before setting it down on the counter.

She glanced nervously around the room, everywhere but at him. "This is awkward, huh?"

"Yeah. I seem to recall that we agreed not to see each other again."

"I know," she said. "And I'm sorry, but the situation has changed."

He folded his arms across his chest and leaned back against the refrigerator. "Which situation is that?"

She took a deep breath and blew it out, then looked him in the eye and said, "The situation that arose when I found out I was pregnant."

Chapter Three

It took a full thirty seconds for the meaning of her words to sink in, and another minute to regain the use of his vocal chords. "Say again?"

"I was surprised, too." She walked across the room to the floor-to-ceiling windows overlooking the shore of Lake Michigan. "Before you ask, I'm sure it's yours. There hasn't been anyone else in a while."

"I wasn't going to ask." The thought had never even occurred to him. She didn't strike him as the type of woman who would try to pin someone else's mistake on him. Though, it wasn't as if he knew her all that well. Geographically he'd memorized her down to the last detail. The way her breasts felt cupped in his hands, the soft swell of her hips. How their bodies had locked together to make a perfect fit.

Personally and intellectually, they were barely more than strangers.

"Well," she asked, finally turning to him. "Aren't you going to say anything?"

"The truth is, I'm a little speechless right now."

"You must have questions."

There were so many questions bouncing around in his head he could barely make sense of them. "You've been to see a doctor? You're sure?"

"Do you think I would fly all the way here from Texas if I wasn't sure?"

Which led to his next question. "How? We used protection."

"I can't explain it, either. But if you're interested in placing blame, go ahead and pin it on me."

If he recalled correctly, they had both been in that room, he just as willingly as she'd been. "Why would I do that? It isn't anyone's fault."

"Actually, it is." She lowered her eyes, toying with the hem of her shirt. "While I had no plan to get pregnant, I walked into that bar with every intention of seducing you."

The corner of his mouth quirked up. Is that

what she thought happened? *She* seduced him? "Is that so?"

She wouldn't meet his eye. "It's dumb really, but I was so mad at you after that interview, I wanted revenge. I wanted a way to prove you wrong. There was obvious chemistry, so I used it to my advantage. I guess the joke was on me."

Maybe he should have been offended; instead, he felt sorry for her. She was beating herself up over something that wasn't her fault. "Miranda, you can't seduce someone who doesn't want to be seduced. You could have danced naked on the table, but unless I was interested, it wouldn't have gotten me into bed with you. And maybe you're forgetting, but I made the first move." He crossed the kitchen to her, cupping her chin in his hand and lifting her face to him. "Let's forget about whose fault this is and figure out what we're going to do."

She nodded, gratitude in her eyes.

Touching her face brought back the memory of that night in the hotel, right before he kissed her. And since he was this close to doing it again, he let his hand drop and backed away.

"How long have you known?"

"A while. I wanted to give myself a couple of weeks to let it sink in before I told you."

"And you're happy?"

"I've always wanted children. It was just unexpected."

He could sympathize.

"How about you?" she asked.

He wasn't sure what he felt yet. He was still having a hard time wrapping his mind around the concept. He'd always planned on a family, too, just not like this. Looks like now he didn't have a choice.

"When?" he asked.

"Right around Christmas."

A Christmas baby.

He was going to be a father.

"Then I guess there's only one thing we can do," he said.

"What's that?"

"We have to get married."

Miranda had had her share of surprises in the past couple of weeks. The first was when she'd looked at her day planner and realized her period was a week late. The second had been when she'd counted back the days to her night with Zack and realized they'd slept together on what was likely her most fertile time of the month. Her third, and she thought final, surprise came when the doctor called, delivering the results of her blood test.

And none of them came close to the whopper he'd just laid on her.

"If that was a joke, it wasn't funny," she told him. Only, he didn't look as if he were joking. She'd never seen him look so dead serious. Of course, she'd never seen him in anything but a suit and tie, either.

Well, that and naked.

"Do you really think I would joke about something like that?" he asked.

"I don't know what to think. I don't really know you, Zack. Which, if you weren't joking, is a pretty good argument why we *shouldn't* get married. I have no objections to you being a part of this baby's life. I'm *relieved* that you want to be. I know that if we try we can work out a plan we both can be comfortable with."

"I don't think you're looking at the big picture," he said, in an infuriatingly patient tone. As though he were addressing a child. Or a moron. Yet somehow he managed not to sound condescending, which was even more frustrating. He was so damned sure of himself. So reasonable.

"That is *all* I've been doing for the past week," she told him. "I've weighed my options. We live in the twenty-first century, where single parenthood is readily accepted."

"Not for me it isn't. It's against everything I believe. I've built my career around family values."

"And I've built mine around being a modern, independent woman. Am I just supposed to marry you and throw that all away?"

"A child should grow up with both parents."

"And our baby will. Just in separate households."

"If you're worried about money, I'll see that you're always taken care of, no matter what."

"Oh, no," she said, shaking her head and narrowing her eyes at him. He was stepping on very dangerous ground. "Don't even go there. Don't think for a minute that you're going to turn me into Suzie Homemaker. I've played that game before and I lost big-time. The only person taking care of me is me."

"So this is all about your career?" he asked, and she could see his patience slipping. He was getting frustrated. But he still hadn't so much as raised his voice.

Would he be like her ex-husband? Would he change after they were married? Would he start calling her stupid and useless? Would he compare her to wives of his friends? Things like, "Dave's wife keeps their house spotless. Why can't you be more like her?" or "Look how thin Mike's wife is. Why don't you lose some weight?"

"Well, isn't that the pot calling the kettle black," she told Zack. "Tell me you're not thinking about the jump in book sales when everyone hears you've reformed a man-hating feminist she-cat."

The corners of his mouth quirked up. "Someone actually called you a man-hating feminist she-cat?"

She shot him a warning look and he wiped the smile from his face. "Saving your career is a lousy reason to get married."

"And it's a lousy reason not to."

"You want a reason why we shouldn't get married? You don't love me and I don't love you. We hardly know each other!"

"How about this for a reason." He cupped a hand behind her head, threading his fingers through her hair and tilted her face up to his. The same aggressive yet gentle approach he'd used that night in the hotel. She knew what he was going to do, and she knew she should stop him. But as his head lowered, as if she were under some sort of spell, her eyes slipped closed instead. And when his lips touched hers, she went weak all over.

Talk about a pushover. Where was her sense of empowerment? The one she talked about in her book. The one every woman was supposed to have. The God-given right, not to mention responsibility, to speak up and say *no*.

Or maybe you had to *want* to say no for that to work.

The kiss went from sweet to passionate in the span of a heartbeat. He tasted like coffee and something sweet, and she was thankful for the breath mint she'd popped in her mouth on the way over from the airport.

He slid one big hand over her backside, pulling her intimately against him, and her brain nearly shut down altogether. She fisted her hands at her sides to keep from touching him.

When he finally pulled away he did it reluctantly, his lips lingering over hers for several seconds, his hands sliding up to her shoulders, then down her arms before he let go and backed away.

"Reason enough?" he asked, his tone deep and lusty.

She attempted a reply, but her voice cracked, so she cleared her throat and tried again. "You know as well as I do that animal attraction isn't enough to make a marriage work."

He gave her that grin, the one that managed to be cocky without actually being cocky. "We connected. You can't deny that."

She wouldn't even try to. And she could see he wasn't going to back down. What did he think— he would kiss and she would melt?

Well, okay, maybe she had melted. That didn't mean he could snap his fingers and tell her to jump and expect her to ask how high. Not in this lifetime. Not even if he asked politely. "It's not going to happen, Zack. I don't want to marry you, and I don't think you want to marry me, either."

"I want to be a part of my child's life."

"And you will be. We'll work out a custody arrangement we can both live with."

"Fatherhood doesn't begin with the birth. I want the whole nine yards. I want to hear the heartbeat at doctor's appointments. I want be there for the ultrasound. I want the baby to bond to the sound of my voice. It would be unfair to deny me that."

He was right. This was as much his child as hers. But he was asking the impossible.

She took a seat at the kitchen table, suddenly feeling exhausted. She thought telling him would be a relief, that it would lift the weight that had been resting on her shoulders. Now she could see that it had only opened the door to more problems that would need solving before she got back to her life. "How can we do that? We live a thousand miles apart."

"We have only one choice." He pulled out the chair next to hers and spun it around, straddling the seat, his arms resting on the low back. It was tough to reconcile the memory of the relationship guru she'd sparred with on the radio, with the real man sitting there in jeans, a T-shirt and bare feet. He looked so *normal*.

"I'm all ears," she said.

"One of us will have to relocate."

Of course, that would be the logical solution. And she could just imagine which of them he expected to pull up roots and move halfway across the country.

But she was in the middle of writing a book. She had piles of research and reference books in her home office that she needed access to. She had an obstetrician she loved. There was simply no way she could uproot her entire life right now.

And she was sure that wasn't what Mr. I-Want-To-Be-A-Part-Of-My-Child's-Life wanted to hear.

"Since my lecture schedule will frequently be taking me on the road, anyway," he continued, "it makes sense that I move to Texas."

Huh?

She was too dumbfounded to speak. She must have heard him wrong.

"You would relocate to be close to me?" she said, to confirm exactly what he was saying.

"Temporarily, yes. At least until the baby is a few months old."

No way it could be that simple. He had to have something up his sleeve. There had to be some sort of condition to go along with his seemingly generous offer. "What's the catch?"

He shrugged. "No catch."

She narrowed her eyes at him. "I'm supposed to believe that you're willing to move across the country to be closer to me and you expect nothing in return?"

"Let me guess. Your ex-husband wasn't so willing to compromise? Or was it an overbearing father?"

Both, actually, but that was none of his business. She shot him a look. "Don't shrink me."

He reciprocated with one of those cocky, but not really cocky, looks. How did he *do* that? "I promise not to shrink you, if you promise not to make assumptions based on experiences you've had with men who aren't me."

Touché. She had to hand it to him, if nothing else he was direct. And fair.

"All I'm asking for, Miranda, is your time. I'd like us to get to know each other. You may be surprised to find that I'm not such a bad guy."

Maybe that was what she was worried about. She didn't want to know. She didn't want to be tempted. Her husband had seemed like a nice guy, too, and look what a disaster that had turned out to be.

But it would be incredibly unfair to deny him the

opportunity to be a part of her pregnancy due to her own feelings of insecurity and self-doubt.

Oh, great, now she was shrinking *herself.* And she was a lawyer for heaven's sake!

"Where would you stay?" she asked.

"I'll find a rental. Preferably one close to your place."

Her practical side, the one that had lived for five years with a husband who kept her on a strict monthly allowance despite a lucrative law practice, cringed. "Won't that be expensive?"

He shrugged, as if it didn't matter either way. And why would it? The guy was an empire. He had produced a library of DVDs, written half a dozen books that had become instant bestsellers, and she could just imagine what he made on the lecture circuit filling countless auditoriums to capacity.

The area where she lived was comfortable, but not exactly upscale, which would probably be what he was looking for, but there were developments not far from her that would probably suit him. Complexes with penthouse apartments and luxury condos. And she was only a twenty-minute drive from downtown Dallas. He would definitely find something cushy enough there.

"I'm sure you could find something close by," she said.

He reached behind him for the pad of paper and pen sitting next to the phone and handed them to her. "Write down your address and I'll have my assistant look into it. I guess you should probably include your phone number while you're at it. So I can reach you."

She was having his baby, and he didn't even know her phone number. This was too weird. The kind of thing she read about in books or saw on television dramas. This kind of thing wasn't supposed to happen in real life. Especially not to her.

As she jotted the information down she wondered what the heck she was getting herself into. Everything was moving so fast, and felt so…final. She had been hoping he would want to be involved with the baby. Weekend visitation at best. But he wanted to be *involved*.

She didn't know if she was ready for this.

She had considered not telling him about the baby, but she didn't doubt her pregnancy would eventually reach the media. Zack was a smart guy. It would take only a very simple equation for him to determine the baby was his.

And for all her talk of being modern and independent, she still knew right from wrong.

Sure, she could raise the baby alone. She had the financial means. But to deny the child a relationship with its father, and vice versa, wouldn't be right.

It was a moot point now. She was here and it was a done deal.

She handed the paper back to him. "What are we going to do about the media? I'm assuming you would prefer this not get out."

"How do you feel about that?" he asked, sounding an awful lot like a shrink.

"I understand. I don't expect you to jeopardize your reputation for the sake of my feelings. And I'm not exactly looking forward to the media attention, either. I won't say anything if you don't."

"Deal," he agreed.

"So, when are we talking? I'm guessing soon."

"As soon as I'm able. When is your next doctor appointment?"

"Three weeks."

He cursed under his breath. "I'll be in California for ten days."

"This early, you won't be missing much."

"Then I guess I'll take the next couple of weeks to tie up some loose ends, and be in Texas after my California trip. That would be, what? Fourth week in June?"

A month seemed so far away, and at the same time it wasn't long enough. A precious month left of her privacy. Her freedom. "This is all so... surreal. I mean, we hardly know each other. We're strangers."

And if that was true, why did she feel as though she knew him somehow?

"So this will give us plenty of time to get acquainted."

Maybe that was what she was worried about. She'd learned from one too many disastrous relationships not to trust her own judgment when it came to finding the wrong kind of man. Because the wrong kind of man for her, unfortunately, was the kind of man she was usually attracted to.

Chapter Four

"Another furniture store truck just pulled up," Lianne, Miranda's next-door neighbor, called from her perch on the couch by the front-room window. She had been sitting there for the past twenty minutes giving Miranda a blow-by-blow of the activity going on at the condo across the street.

Miranda stood around the corner in the kitchen, fixing herself a cup of tea and a plate of saltines, hoping it might ease the nausea brewing in her stomach. This was the third morning in a row that she'd woken feeling sick.

She knew that technically, morning sickness was

a good thing. It meant her body was producing enough hormones to sustain a healthy pregnancy. That didn't make her feel any better when she was kneeling to the porcelain gods, yacking up her breakfast. From now on it was tea and crackers every morning until her stomach settled.

"They're unloading the furniture!" Lianne squealed. She was like this whenever someone new moved into the complex. Fresh meat, she liked to say.

Like Miranda, she was divorced. Bitterly divorced. But always in the market for a temporary distraction. She'd divorced her most recent temporary distraction three months ago.

"So far so good," she reported. "Nothing kid related. No toys or baby furniture. Nothing too feminine, either. Could be a single man."

The kettle began to whistle, and she poured boiling water into her cup. "You know that the first rule of dating is to *never* get involved with a neighbor," she called back.

Lianne knew. She'd read Miranda's book. But she still slipped back into her old ways from time to time. Hence her three ex-husbands—the latest of whom still lived around the corner.

"There's no harm in looking," she called back.

Miranda carried her tea and crackers into the

front room. She set them on the coffee table and eased herself into the recliner where she'd been spending most of her mornings sacked out in her pajamas in front of the television.

Lianne sat curled up on the couch across the room, her nose practically touching the window. "Don't you want to see?"

Miranda didn't care about anything but making the nausea go away. "I'll look when I can safely move."

She momentarily peeled her eyes from the window to shoot Miranda a sympathetic look. "Still feeling sick, huh?"

"It'll pass," she said, nibbling the edge of a cracker. It was a catch-22. If she didn't eat, she felt sicker, and if she ate too much, that was even worse. The trick was finding just the right balance.

So far, no luck.

"Just be happy you're not like I was with Brandon," Lianne said, referring to her nineteen-year-old son, who was currently in Houston attending college. "Sick as a dog from the day I got pregnant to the minute he was born." She turned back to the window. "Oh, crud. We have baby stuff. They're unloading a box with what looks like a crib...yep it's a crib, all right. And here comes the changing table."

"It'll be nice to have a new family in the complex." Miranda placed a hand over her still-flat stomach. "Someone for the baby to play with when he or she is old enough."

Lianne sighed and turned from the window. "Have you decided if you want to find out the baby's sex beforehand?"

"I'm not sure yet. On one hand, I love a good surprise, on the other, I could be more prepared if I knew."

"What about the baby's father? Does he want to know?"

Lianne knew the basic events surrounding Miranda's pregnancy, but not the identity of the man involved. No one knew. Most people, including Miranda's family, didn't even know she was pregnant.

She knew exactly what people would say, what her family would think, and while she had stopped playing by their rules a long time ago, she just didn't have the energy to deal with them right now. She was giving herself permission to be selfish for a while.

Miranda sipped her tea. "We haven't decided yet."

And not for lack of debate. Since her return from Chicago nearly a month ago, she'd spoken to Zack daily. His insatiable curiosity sometimes kept them on the line for an hour or more. And though at first she figured it would rapidly become annoying, now she didn't mind so much. After all, what expectant woman didn't love talking about her pregnancy?

"Well, I think it's pretty cool that he's moving here all the way from Chicago to be close to you. I can't wait to meet him."

Which could be a problem. Especially if they planned to keep this from the media. Zack was an empire. If he came to her condo, someone was bound to recognize him, and eventually, someone would talk.

The more she thought about it, the more complicated it was sounding.

"The woman we thought was the decorator is back," Lianne said, nose to the window again. "She must be the wife, although I don't see a baby anywhere."

Miranda set her half-full cup down. She'd managed that and two crackers. She leaned her head back and closed her eyes, waiting for the sickness to pass.

"We've got a black car pulling up to the curb. Holy cow. It's vintage. A Mustang, I think. In mint condition. And it's a guy behind the wheel."

Miranda rocked gently, only half listening. She was starting to feel better. The crackers and tea were working.

"He's getting out. Wow. Talk about tall, dark and handsome," Lianne said wistfully. "And he's got a body to die for. Come here, you need to see this guy."

"Not yet." She couldn't move yet. If she got up

too soon, she would just get sick all over again. And honestly, she didn't care what the new family across the street looked like.

"He's got to be at least six-one. Maybe even taller. He's wearing a baseball cap, but I can tell his hair is short and dark. Dark brown, I think. He's wearing cut-off jeans, a T-shirt and sandals. Very casual. I'm guessing midtwenties. Thirty tops."

She could feel the nausea subsiding. Little by little.

"His wife just came outside. They're chatting. You would think he would give her a kiss or hug or *something.*"

"Maybe he doesn't like public displays of affection," Miranda said, feeling obligated to contribute to the conversation. She actually appreciated Lianne's morning visits. It helped keep her mind off how miserable she felt.

A writer like Miranda, she worked from a home office, so it wasn't uncommon for her to drop by three or four times a day. Sometimes, when she developed a case of writer's block, she would even bring her laptop over and set up shop on Miranda's couch. She claimed the change of atmosphere would sometimes get the creative juices flowing.

"He's smiling," Lianne reported. "Oh, yeah, he's a hunk. Major beefcake."

The word "beef" made Miranda's stomach lurch.

"I wish he would lose the shades so I could see his eyes. And what's this? Hold the phones...*he's kissing her cheek!* Very brief and polite. No way this woman is his wife."

"That doesn't mean he doesn't have one," Miranda pointed out. "Maybe she's already inside unpacking."

"She's handing him something. Keys I think. Now she's going back inside the condo. The beef-cake is looking around, scoping out the cul-de-sac."

Miranda fought the bile rising up from her stomach. "If you say beef one more time, I'm going to hurl."

"Now he's looking across the street...oh, damn, I think I've been discovered."

"Serves you right," Miranda said, not opening her eyes. "That's what you get for being nosy."

"I'm not nosy. I'm observant. And let's not forget whose window I'm looking out of. He'll probably just assume it's you."

Swell. Just what she needed, her new neighbors thinking she was a snoop.

"He's walking back to his car...no wait, he walked past it, and he's crossing the street. He's coming this way."

"That's not funny," Miranda said.

"I'm not trying to be funny. He's really crossing

the street. And, oh my God, he *is* a hunk. Older than I thought, though. More like his midthirties."

A teeny, tiny alarm rang in her head. Tall, midthirties, a hunk.

No way.

"Now he's walking up your driveway."

The alarm grew louder, or was it just a ringing in her ears? She was starting to feel light-headed. "I'm not buying it, Lianne."

"He's walking up the steps to the porch…"

Sure he was.

Lianne was just messing with her head. She liked to do that.

"…stopping to look at the flowers in the urn. *Picking* one of the flowers! Boy does this guy have nerve."

She would drag this out as long as humanly possible.

"Stepping up to the door…"

The doorbell rang.

Miranda's eyes flew open.

Lianne was looking at her. "Well? Aren't you going to get it?"

Miranda looked down at her attire. "I'm in my pajamas. I haven't even brushed my teeth yet."

"Okay," Lianne, said with a sigh, rising from the couch. "I'll get it."

As she walked to the front door, Miranda's nausea returned full force. He was probably just coming by to use the phone, or borrow sugar. She was sure she didn't know him.

As Lianne reached for the doorknob Miranda squeezed her eyes shut, as if not seeing it wouldn't make it real. But she had a bad feeling about this.

The bile was rising again. Working it's way up, burning a path through the lining of her throat.

She heard the door open, heard a deep voice. *His* voice.

"I'm looking for Miranda Reed," it said.

"Can I tell her who you might be?" Lianne asked, her voice stern, yet curious.

"Tell her it's Zack."

Zack had heard of people turning green, but always assumed it was a figure of speech.

It wasn't.

When he walked into Miranda's condo and saw her sitting there, she looked like the creature from the green lagoon.

It was the first time anyone had looked at him, then promptly run to the bathroom to toss their cookies.

"Feeling better now?" he asked from the bathroom doorway.

Miranda groaned.

She half sat, half sprawled on the tile floor wearing pink silk pajamas, her arms draped over the bowl. Her long, dark hair was pulled back but a few wispy strands stuck to her forehead and cheek. "Someone kill me now."

"Is there anything I can get you?"

She moaned and laid her head on her arm. "Have you got a gun?"

That one made him smile. "I was thinking more along the lines of a damp cloth or a glass of water."

She gazed up at him, her eyes watery and bloodshot. "I know exactly what you're thinking."

"What am I thinking?"

"You're looking at me now, remembering when you proposed, and saying to yourself, thank God she said no."

She couldn't be more wrong. "Why would I be thinking that?"

"I've seen my reflection in the toilet bowl. You can't tell me I don't look like a beast."

"I've never met anyone who looks good hanging over a toilet being sick. I promise not to hold it against you."

"What happened to Lianne?"

"She left. She wants you to call her when you're feeling better."

Miranda just bet she did. She had to be going nuts over there wondering what the heck was going on. "Does she know who you are?"

"I told her I'm a friend of yours from Chicago."

"Yep, she knows."

"*What* does she know exactly?"

"That you're the baby's father. She just doesn't know *who* you are. At least, I hope she doesn't." She sat up and took a few shallow breaths. "I think I'm feeling better now."

"You ready to get up?"

"I think so."

He stepped into the bathroom and held out a hand to give her a boost from the floor. She grabbed it and rose slowly to her feet. She wavered a second, gripping his fingers. "Where do you want to go?" he asked.

"The recliner."

With a hand resting on her lower back for stability, he walked her out to the chair. She sat down, leaned back and closed her eyes. She wasn't looking so green any longer. It was the first time he'd seen her with no makeup, and he sort of liked her without it. She looked softer. And younger. Maybe even a little bit vulnerable.

And he intended to take care of her. This was exactly what he'd meant when he told her he wanted to be involved. He wanted to be a part of the *entire* process. Even the unpleasant parts.

He noticed her cup on the table. "Would you like more tea?"

"You don't have to take care of me."

"I know I don't."

For a second he thought she might argue, then she must have decided she didn't have the energy. "Tea would be great. With a teaspoon of honey." Eyes still closed, she gestured in the direction of the kitchen. "It's in the cabinet above the coffeemaker."

He grabbed her cup from the table. "I'll find it."

Like the rest of the condo, the kitchen was very clean and organized. That was one thing they obviously had in common. Clutter drove him nuts. His mother never had time for housework. She'd worked long hours, and when she finally did get home, cooking and cleaning were pretty low on her list of priorities.

She would open a bottle of wine, park herself in front of the television and chain-smoke until his father got home. How much she drank depended on how late he was out. He had a lot of evening "meetings" and often didn't breeze in until after midnight.

Sometimes it was one bottle, other nights two. On a good night, she would pass out before his father returned, sparing Zack and his younger brother

Richard from being jolted awake to the sound of raised voices. To hear his mother's slurred accusations, and his father's halfhearted, lame excuses.

On a bad night, the police got involved.

His mother's second and third marriages hadn't been much better.

He put the kettle on, dumped out the stale tea and fixed her a fresh cup. When he walked back into the family room she looked much better. In fact, he would go so far as to say she was glowing. Her cheeks were rosy and her eyes bright. She looked... maternal.

He handed her the cup, making sure she had a steady grip before letting go. "You look as though you're feeling better."

"I am." She sipped the tea and smiled. "It's perfect. Thanks."

He took a seat on the couch and glanced out the window. The moving van was still there, but Taylor, his sister-in-law and relocation coordinator, assured him she would have everything in order by lunchtime.

Miranda took another sip of her tea and set the cup down. "Nice place across the street."

"Very nice," he agreed. Smaller than he was used to, but it would suffice.

"Tell me you didn't really just move there."

Unfortunately he couldn't do that. "I told you I wanted to be closer."

"Yeah, but right across the street? Are you nuts?"

"Not the last time I checked."

"We've talked every day for a month and you never once thought to mention it? I was thinking you would move to Dallas, or Fort Worth, even. I thought you would at least have to get in the car and *drive* to see me. This could be incredibly...*awkward*."

"It doesn't have to be." It wasn't as if he hadn't expected this. He knew there would be an adjustment period while she grew used to the idea of having him around. He didn't doubt that everything would work out. Given time, she would see things his way.

She may have been strong willed and determined, but so was he.

"That's easy for you to say," she snapped back. "You get to leave whenever you want. You can go back to Chicago or lecture. I'm stuck here. All my work, all my research material is in this house."

"You make it sound as though I'm holding you prisoner. And I do have to point out that right now, you could use my help. At least until the morning sickness passes."

She didn't look convinced. "You don't think it will be weird, us living so close?"

Across the street wasn't close enough as far as

he was concerned. He was determined, by the time this baby was born, to convince her to marry him. Preferably sooner than later. The only way he could do that was to spend as much time with her as possible.

He had every intention of seducing her, as well, although that part of the plan might have to wait until she was feeling better.

"You should have talked to me about this first," she said. "We should have discussed it."

"We did discuss it. I said I was moving closer, you said okay. In fact, at the time, I thought you sounded relieved that I was the one doing the relocating."

He could see that she wanted to argue but couldn't deny he was right. She *had* been relieved. And had he used that to his advantage? Maybe so, but he was only doing what was best for her and the baby. She needed him around, even if she wasn't willing to admit it yet.

Instead, she tried a different angle. "I thought you wanted to keep this quiet. You don't think people are going to see us together and catch on?"

"The house is under a different name, and I have my disguise." He plucked the sunglasses from the front of his shirt and put them on then he tugged the baseball cap low over his eyes. "See."

"I still recognize you."

He ignored her cynicism. "Once I let my beard grow out, no one will know who I am."

"You look *that* different with a beard?"

"You'd be surprised."

She didn't look as though she believed him. "What will you do when you lecture?"

"Shave it off before I leave, then grow it back when I'm home."

"Is the car part of the disguise, too? You seem more like a Mercedes kinda guy."

"You like it? It was my dream car when I was kid. I thought it would fit with the persona."

She closed her eyes and sighed, as if gathering her patience. "How long is your lease?"

"On the car?"

"No, on the house."

"I'm not leasing it."

Her eyes opened. "Renting?"

He shook his head. "I bought it. I figure, after the baby is born I'll need a place to stay when I come to visit. What better place than across the street?"

It took her a minute to digest that one, and he could swear she was starting to look a little green again. Was the idea of having him around really so revolting? Or was it that she felt her independence was being threatened?

"Wouldn't you rather have something bigger? Something in a higher-class neighborhood? I'm sure there's a penthouse apartment in Dallas with your name written all over it."

"But I don't want to live in Dallas." The truth was he had no intention of staying in the condo any longer than necessary. He'd bought it more as a gesture of faith. So she would understand that he was serious.

When he left Texas, whether that was before or after the baby was born, he had every intention of taking Miranda with him. Even if he couldn't talk her into marrying him, he wanted her and his child close. He would find some way to talk her into moving to Chicago.

And if that didn't work, he might just be looking for a more permanent residence in Texas. Maybe that penthouse in Dallas she mentioned.

Throughout his childhood, his father had been invisible, and Zack couldn't deny it had left deep scars. Zack planned to be around for his son or daughter. He would be there to see every new tooth and hear the first words. He would be around to kiss scraped knees and wipe away tears. He would be the dad who walked his child to school and attended band concerts.

For him it was no imposition, unlike his father,

who saw his duty to his family like a lead anchor weighing him down.

Given the time and lots of patience, he was quite sure he would wear Miranda down. There was no other option. Eventually he would convince her that his way was the right way.

Chapter Five

Miranda's eyes fluttered open. The curtains were drawn and the room dim, and the throw from the back of the couch had been draped over her legs.

She must have dozed off.

She sat up and rubbed the sleep from her eyes. For a second, she thought it had all been a crazy dream. Or a nightmare. Maybe Zack really hadn't moved in across the street.

But beside her on the table sat a cold cup of tea and next to that was a note that read: "Across the street if you need me." He'd included his cell phone number, home number and address. As if she could forget where he lived.

Sheesh!

It looked as though this particular nightmare was just beginning.

She had fallen into this trap more than once, her life subjugated by overbearing, controlling men. First with her father and brothers, and then her ex-husband. It hadn't been easy clawing her way out from under their collective thumbs. But she was stronger now.

She needed to tell Zack, in no uncertain terms, that she would be the one calling the shots this time.

She sat very still for a moment, trying to gauge the level of nausea. A little twinge maybe, but nothing she couldn't handle. Very slowly, and with great caution, she sat up. And her stomach growled. She was actually hungry, meaning that for today, at least, the worst of it had passed.

She fixed herself a few slices of toast and a fresh cup of tea. When she managed to keep that down without incident, she added fruit and cottage cheese to her plate.

Afterward, she took a hot shower and got dressed. She considered working for a while, but she knew she would get nothing accomplished until she settled things with her new "neighbor."

She debated with herself about taking the time to

apply makeup, then decided she didn't have the energy. It wasn't as though Zack hadn't seen her looking worse. And besides, she had no reason to impress him or try to soften him up. On the contrary, he was going to learn that she was not a woman to mess with.

At least, not anymore.

It was nearly 2:00 p.m. by the time she stepped out the door. She considered popping in next door for a second, but she hadn't quite decided what she wanted to tell Lianne. Besides, avoiding the situation with Zack wasn't bound to make it go away.

Instead, she crossed the street. The summer sun beat down, hot and ruthless, and she could swear she felt steam rising from her still-damp hair. Sweat beaded her upper lip by the time she reached his driveway.

The moving van was gone, and Zack's second-hand car sat in the street. She stepped up to the porch and knocked on the door. From inside she could hear the heavy beat of music and the muffled whine of a guitar riff.

She checked the address to be sure she hadn't accidentally walked up to the wrong door. He didn't strike her as the hard-rock type, but there were probably a lot of things that she didn't know about him.

It was a good thing his next-door neighbors both

worked during the day. The walls here weren't exactly soundproof.

When he didn't answer, she tried ringing the bell.

The door opened, and instead of Zack, the woman Miranda had seen coming and going regularly for the past two weeks stood there.

"Can I help you?" she asked. She was tall, wispy and beautiful in a soft, delicate way. Like a fragile flower. Yet poised and sturdy somehow.

Miranda had the sudden nightmarish realization that this woman could be Zack's girlfriend. Or… *gulp*…his wife. Maybe one of many.

What if he had women all over the country? A girl in every port he visited on the lecture circuit. For all she knew he could have illegitimate kids all over the place, too.

As rapidly as the idea formed, it evaporated away into the heat.

What man would be dumb enough to bring his girlfriend to the house across the street from his pregnant mistress?

Oh, God. Is that what she was? Someone's *mistress?* Had she sunk that low?

Recognition lit the woman's face. "You must be Miranda."

"Yes, but—"

With a delighted little gasp and a warm smile,

she grasped Miranda's hands and squeezed them. "How wonderful to finally meet you! Come inside! It's hot as the devil out there. I don't know how you Texans can stand it."

She all but dragged Miranda over the threshold, but Miranda was too stunned to resist. Who the heck was she? And why did she know who Miranda was? Wasn't this supposed to be a covert operation? A secret? Why bother with a disguise if he was going to go telling everyone where he was?

"I'm Taylor Jameson," she said.

"Jameson?" His sister? Or, oh, God, maybe she *was* his wife. Maybe his relationship-guru persona was just a front, and in truth he was some sort of twisted cult leader. A bigamist.

Taylor must have recognized Miranda's abject horror, because she added, "Zack's sister-in-law."

Miranda breathed a sigh of relief and plastered a smile on her face. "Nice to meet you."

"I take it Zack never mentioned me."

Miranda didn't know what to say. She didn't want to hurt Taylor's feelings, but really all she knew about Zack was that he had one brother. When they talked it was usually about the pregnancy or work. Rarely did they get personal.

"It's okay," Taylor said. "Zack is a very private person."

"I'm beginning to notice that."

Apparently, Zack trusted her to keep the situation in confidence. If Taylor even knew what the situations was.

What had Zack told her?

"Aren't you just adorable!" she said, looking Miranda up and down, still clutching her hands, her grip firm yet delicate. Normally a comment like that would have come off as condescending, but Taylor was so excited, the words felt genuine. "I've been pumping Zack for information, but you know how men can be."

That lack of information had to be the explanation for her enthusiasm. Had she known the truth, Miranda doubted she would be so warm and friendly. She wondered what she did know. Or more to the point what she *didn't* know.

"I wanted to introduce myself sooner, but Zack made me promise not to. He wanted you to be surprised when he moved in."

Oh, did he? Well, he'd succeeded. "I'm definitely surprised."

"Maybe I'm being too forward, but I would absolutely love to throw you a baby shower."

A shower? So, she knew about the baby.

Miranda opened her mouth to respond, but she didn't know what to say. Weren't they getting ahead of themselves? She had barely gotten used to the idea that she was pregnant.

This was all moving way too fast. She could almost feel the walls closing in on her. That sickening sensation of claustrophobia.

"If I'm overstepping my boundaries, just say so. I tend to do that. I just love planning parties. And I love babies even more."

Outside, a car horn sounded and she let go of Miranda's hands. "Oh, damn, that's my ride! I was hoping we would have more time to chat, but I have a flight to catch. Richard is anxious to meet you, too, so we'll probably be in town soon. Maybe we could all go out to dinner."

"Uh, yeah, sure."

"It was a pleasure meeting you, Miranda." She pumped Miranda's hand again, then grabbed her purse from the entryway table. "I hope we'll talk again soon."

"Me, too," Miranda said, although she had barely gotten a word in edgewise.

The horn sounded a second time. "Coming, coming!" she chattered with a flutter of her hand, then glanced in the direction of the stairs. "Do me a favor and tell Zack I said goodbye. Tell him to call if he needs anything."

With one last waggle of her fingers she was out

the door, a tornado of energy, and though the conversation had been one-sided, Miranda felt a little breathless. Two minutes with Taylor and she was exhausted.

She turned and looked around the front room. Zack certainly spared no expense. It screamed, "professionally decorated."

The walls were freshly painted in warm, neutral beiges. The furniture and decorations were masculine enough to suit a man, without overpowering. The effect was warm and inviting.

Miranda followed the music up the stairs to the spare bedroom that in her condo she used as an office. She stepped through the doorway and found herself surrounded by soft pastels, plush carpet and expensive-looking baby furniture.

On the dresser sat one of those nifty little portable MP3 players attached to a speaker set that played amazingly loud and clear for their size.

In the middle of the room knelt Zack, singing at the top of his lungs in perfect pitch with Robert Plant, assembling, of all things, a crib.

It created a picture so adorable, had she been an emotional woman, it might have brought tears to her eyes. As it was, she couldn't help smiling, or fight the warm fuzzy feelings building in her heart.

She might not know him very well, that was

painfully obvious, but what she did know, she liked. Probably too much for her own good. She had to remind herself that some men were not what they seemed.

She wasn't quite ready to trust him.

She rapped on the door frame. "Knock, knock."

He turned, and when he saw it was her, a smile lit his face. Oh, man, was he cute. Her heart did a quick back-and-forth shimmy.

"You don't strike me as the Zeppelin type," she shouted over the music.

He reached over and turned the volume down. "There's a lot about me you don't know."

Wasn't that the truth. "I know you have a sister-in-law with an excess of energy."

He grinned. He'd lost the baseball cap and suffered a mild case of hat hair. "I take it you met Taylor."

"She said to tell you goodbye and to call if you need anything. And she offered to throw me a baby shower."

He rose to his feet, tall and wide. Imposing, yet completely unthreatening. Superior, but humble.

How did he manage that?

"Sorry about that. She sometimes gets a little *too* enthusiastic. She means well, though. And if you're worried, our secret is safe with her."

"She said she and Richard would be visiting soon, and we could all go out to dinner. Are you and your brother close?"

"Pretty close."

Apparently, he had no plans to elaborate. And that was probably a good thing. The less she knew about him, the less likely she was to get attached.

She gestured to the partially assembled crib. "It looks as though you've been busy."

He turned to review his handiwork. "You like it?"

"You don't think it's a bit…premature?"

He shrugged. "Nothing wrong with being prepared. You're looking as though you feel better."

"Much. Thanks for taking care of me this morning."

He shrugged as if it was no big deal. But she wasn't used to people taking care of her. Especially not a man. And she couldn't help but suspect he had ulterior motives. That he was softening her up so she would let her guard down. It wouldn't be the first time.

"I was hoping you might have some time to talk. But if you're busy, I can come by later." The second the words were out she wished them back. That was the old Miranda talking. The one who put everyone else's needs, everyone's feelings, before her own.

As independent as she'd become, confrontations

still made her uncomfortable. Maybe deep down she wasn't as confident and in control as she liked to believe. And that was definitely something she needed to work on.

"I'm never too busy for you," he said. That should have been a good thing, but instead it made her feel even more claustrophobic. "Let's go downstairs. I could use a cold beer."

He gestured to the door and she preceded him out. They walked downstairs and he led her to a kitchen that looked very similar to her own, just more expensive. Top-of-the-line appliances and granite countertops. New, solid-wood cabinets and ceramic tile floors.

The word that came to mind was luxurious.

"Would you like something? Water? Juice?"

"Water would be good."

He opened the fully stocked side-by-side refrigerator and pulled out a bottled water and an imported beer. "What did you want to talk about?"

"The...*situation.*"

"Which situation would that be?" He cracked the seal on the water and handed it to her. Then he popped open his beer and took a swig.

"You living across the street from me."

Again with the shrug. "What's the problem?"

He wasn't fooling her for a second. He knew

exactly what the problem was, and pretending it didn't exist wasn't going to make it disappear.

"I think we need to set a few boundaries."

"Boundaries?"

"So things don't get…unmanageable." Come, on Miranda. Stop being so polite and just say what you mean.

She sipped her water, wishing it was a margarita or a double martini. Alcohol always made her feel bolder, more brave. Part of the reason she was in the mess in the first place.

On second thought, maybe a drink would be a bad idea.

"I need space. I feel…smothered."

He looked more intrigued than insulted. Maybe even a little bit amused. "I've been here a few hours and already you're telling me to back off?"

If he was trying to make her feel guilty, it wasn't going to work. Or at the very least she wouldn't let it show.

"I could live twenty miles from here and I guarantee you wouldn't be seeing any less of me than you will with me staying right across the street."

"It just feels as though this is all moving too fast."

He took a swallow of beer. "What would you like me to do about it?"

Good question. She couldn't very well ask him

to move back to Chicago. And that was 29 percent of the problem.

Well, she *could* ask. But there was no guarantee he would listen. In fact, she was pretty darned sure he wouldn't. And it wouldn't be fair. This was his baby, too.

"Respect my privacy for starters. I don't want you to get the impression that it's okay to just pop over whenever you feel like it. I would appreciate a phone call first. Especially during the day when I'm working."

"Are you trying to tell me that I overstepped my boundaries this morning?"

He didn't mince words, did he? It was a quality she admired. Probably because she lacked it herself. "As I said before, I appreciated your help, but I can take care of myself."

"I would never question your competence, Miranda. And I'm not here with the intention of disrupting your life. We're having a baby together and I want to be a part of it. It's as simple as that."

Was he serious, or just humoring her? She couldn't tell. She felt torn between wanting to believe him, wanting to trust him and the reality of her past experiences. In her world, men were never what they appeared to be.

"You, on the other hand—" he fished a set of

keys out of the front pocket of his shorts and gave them to her "—are welcome to stop by whenever you feel like it. There's a key for the condo, the car and my apartment in Chicago. Just in case."

"I can't accept these." She tried to hand them back, but he gently pushed her hand away.

"Consider it a gesture of goodwill."

Goodwill? After she had just bluntly told him to back off? Could he really be that easygoing? That generous? There had to be a catch. Some condition he wasn't revealing. This had "messy and complicated" written all over it.

"What if one of us wants to go out on a date?" she asked. "Suppose you have a woman over and I pop in unannounced? You don't think that will be uncomfortable?"

"I have no intention of dating anyone while I'm staying here."

"What if *I* want to date? How do you know I don't already have a boyfriend?"

Again the subtle grin. The one that made her head feel swimmy. Did he know how cute he looked when he did that?

"This boyfriend has no problem with the fact that you're having another man's baby?"

She shot him a look. "My point is, we don't know each other at all."

"And the only way we'll get to know each other is by spending time together. With me living right across the street, think how quick the process will be."

She hated that he was able to make everything sound so logical, when deep down the whole thing just felt…icky. Or maybe the real problem was she liked Zack. Really liked him, and she was afraid that if she spent too much time with him, his real personality would emerge and her illusions of the man she hoped he was would be shattered.

She wanted him to be as wonderful as he appeared, and at the same time she knew it was incredibly unlikely. But at the very least, she did believe he was honest.

"If this is going to work, you have to promise you'll give me space."

"Whatever you need," he said without batting an eye. "I promise."

Wow, that was easy.

Too easy.

She had a bad feeling about this.

Chapter Six

Being the observant man that he was, Zack immediately picked up on Miranda's wariness. "You look as though you don't believe me."

"I am skeptical," she admitted.

"Then perhaps we should make it official." He extended a hand for her to shake.

She would much rather see it in writing, in an ironclad contract with his name penned in his own blood. But she supposed a handshake deal would have to suffice.

She met him halfway, felt his large, warm hand

swallow hers up. His grip was firm without being overbearing. Intimate, yet platonic.

Damn, he was good.

That grin curled his mouth, hovering somewhere between amused and carnal, and she could swear his eyes darkened a shade. He was giving her that simmering, sexy, come-and-get-me look that had made her knees go weak that evening in the hotel bar.

Uh-oh.

"Don't look at me like that."

One eyebrow tipped up the slightest bit. "Like what?"

"You know exactly what I mean." She tried to tug her hand free, but he tightened his grip just enough to keep her trapped. "You're giving me the eyes."

"The eyes?"

"Yeah, so just stop right now." No doubt he was doing it on purpose. He probably thought he could soften her up. Make her go all mushy-brained.

Which she was.

She tugged again, but he didn't loosen his grip.

The grin widened a fraction. "I have no idea what you're talking about."

Still clutching her hand, he stepped close. Actually, it wasn't so much a step as it was a *lean*. She only knew that he wasn't standing as far away as he was a second ago.

She felt her palm beginning to sweat and her heart did a tap routine across the walls of her chest. She caught the subtle scent of his aftershave over the new paint smell, could swear she felt heat rolling off him in an ebb and flow as natural as the ocean tide. And, oh, boy, he had that look, the one men got right before they kissed a woman.

The same one he had right before he'd kissed her the last time in his kitchen.

She narrowed her eyes and gave him her best don't-mess-with-me look. "Don't even think about it, pal."

Again with the innocent look. "Think about what?"

"Kissing me." She gave another tug, but her hand didn't budge. If she pulled any harder and he did let go, she would end up on her butt on the shiny new tile floor.

"What makes you think that I want to kiss you?"

She was so not falling for this innocent act. "This relationship guru I once sparred with on the radio was quite adamant about the fact that couples should be in a committed relationship before they indulge in sins of the flesh."

If she was hoping to insult him, it hadn't worked. The smile never drifted from his face. If anything, he looked even more amused.

His thumb trailed lightly across the inside of her wrist and she felt herself shiver. Why did he have to do that? And why didn't she make him stop?

Because it felt good, that's why.

"First off, I never once referred to making love as 'sins of the flesh.' And second, as far as I'm concerned, I *am* in a committed relationship."

"This is going to be complicated enough without us getting…involved."

"Define *involved*."

"Sex, Zack."

"Yeah, but think how much fun it could be."

She didn't doubt that for a second. But that kind of fun is what had gotten them in this mess in the first place. "I'm serious. It's not going to happen. It never should have happened the first time."

Slowly, reluctantly, as though he was savoring every last bit of contact, he let her hand slip from his.

"How about dinner tonight," he said. "Would you at least share a meal with me?"

"Is this a meal I have to cook? Because I don't do the domestic goddess thing."

"I did notice that your refrigerator looked a little…light. A nutritious diet is…"

He trailed off when he saw the warning look she was spearing his way. "You so don't want to go there."

"I'll cook," he said.

"Really?"

"Really."

"No carryout or frozen dinners?"

"Nope. Just home-cooked food."

A man who cooked.

How novel.

In all the time she had been married to her ex, she never once saw him use the stove. Not even to boil water for tea. The kitchen had been her room, and it had been her responsibility to have a hot meal on the table every night when he got home from work, regardless of how many hours she herself had worked. After all, her career was only temporary, or so he seemed to believe.

She knew now how wrong it had been of her to be dishonest. To delude him into thinking that she shared his family values. She just kept thinking that one day he would change. He would wake up and realize they weren't living in the nineteenth century and it was okay for a woman to have a career and a family. That she could be an equal.

Unfortunately, that change had never come. Instead of becoming more open-minded and liberal, he'd grown more chauvinistic and controlling.

"What sounds good?" Zack asked. "I make a mean lasagna."

Her salivary glands went into overdrive and she had to swallow to keep from drooling.

"I could eat lasagna," she said casually, while inside she was jumping up and down with joy. Lasagna was only one of her favorite foods in the history of time. Her mother's nana had immigrated to the U.S. from Sicily in the twenties, and though Miranda barely remembered her, she had inherited her appreciation for Italian cuisine.

And since she rarely bothered to go all-out on dinner for one—the guy at the noodle place around the corner knew her by name—a well-rounded meal would be a pleasant change of pace.

"How does six o'clock sound?" he asked.

"I have a lot of work to catch up on. Make it seven and you've got a deal."

"Seven it is."

Okay, then.

Dinner she could handle. Dinner was safe. If she was real lucky, it meant a night of good food, intelligent conversation and a table between them to thwart any unsolicited hanky-panky from his end.

"I look forward to it," she added.

Zack grinned. "You know what I'm looking forward to?"

Why did she get the feeling she didn't want to know? "What?"

He flashed her that look again, the one that made her go all mushy-brained. "Dessert."

There was a note taped to Miranda's front door when she got home, scrawled in Lianne's barely legible handwriting: "Gone for the rest of the day. Hot date. Won't be home until late—I hope. We'll talk tomorrow."

The missed-call light on her phone was flashing when she walked in the door. She checked the caller ID and saw that it was her writing partner, Ivy Madison. Though they only lived twenty minutes from each other, they talked by phone nearly every afternoon to compare notes or work through any problems they might have been having with the book. They kept each other on track that way.

Lately, with Miranda's morning sickness and the fling Ivy had been having with her ex-husband, they'd both fallen a bit behind schedule.

She picked up the cordless and dialed her number. Ivy answered on the first ring.

"You wouldn't believe the day I'm having," Miranda said.

"Miranda, we need to talk."

She knew instantly by the tone of Ivy's voice that something was wrong. She just hoped Dillon, Ivy's ex, hadn't broken her heart again. It had taken an enormous leap of faith for Ivy to trust him again. It had been their messy divorce that had prompted Ivy to coauthor the first book with Miranda.

Both of them having endured heart-wrenchingly painful divorces, the project had been more therapeutic than financially motivated. But since its release, it had been topping the bestseller lists. It had been disturbing to discover the staggering number of women who had endured, or were presently experiencing, painful divorces.

Which was why, with very few exceptions, both Ivy and Miranda vehemently believed women were better off staying single. It was the element they had based their entire book and the follow-up book on.

"What's wrong?" Miranda asked. "Did Dillon do something stupid? Do we need to key his Bentley? Toilet paper his mansion? Put sugar in the fuel tank of his Learjet?"

"No, no, nothing like that. I just…I…"

"What is it?"

"I'm not sure how to say this, so I'm just going to say it. Dillon and I are getting married."

"Married?" Ivy was getting married? To her ex-husband? If she had said that she was getting gender reassignment surgery, Miranda couldn't have been more stunned. It was one thing to have a casual fling with an ex. But to marry him?

"I know what you're thinking," Ivy said.

"Are you nuts?"

"I honestly think this is the first sane thing I've done in a long time. I love him. I think I've always loved him. He makes me happy."

The fact that she was so sure, so blindsided by her ex's charm, added a whole new level of creepiness to the idea. "Of course he does! You're euphoric from all the great sex. But if I had a dime for every time I heard you say great sex does not equal a great marriage, I would be drinking piña coladas on a beach in Maui."

"I was hoping you would be happy for me," Ivy said softly.

Happy?

She couldn't be serious. Ivy was a psychologist, for pity's sake. She had counseled countless women who'd been burned more than once by the same man. "Sure, everything is roses and sunshine now, but how will you feel in six months when the novelty wears off and he turns back into the jerk you divorced?"

"He's not the man he was ten years ago."

"Excuse me? Not the man he used to be? You've said it yourself a million times. Men don't change. Not deep down where it counts."

"I know I did. But Miranda, I was wrong."

A dark and disturbing sensation slithered over

her, and a feeling of dread settled in her gut. She sensed a disaster coming on. "You better not let the publisher hear you talking that way. We have a book to finish. I'm assuming this reunion marriage isn't going to happen until after the release."

There was a long, unsettling pause, then Ivy said, "Um, about that…"

Miranda's heart sunk. "What?"

"I can't do it."

"Can't do what?" she asked, even though she already knew what was coming.

"I can't preach to women about staying single, then turn around and get married."

Miranda felt sick to her stomach, and her head began to spin so hard and fast she felt dizzy. Ivy was going to abandon her? "So you're just going to quit?"

"Not exactly."

A moment of silence from Ivy's end followed, and Miranda's heart slid a little lower in her chest. How much worse could this possibly get?

"I'm not quitting," Ivy told her. "I need to publish a book of my own, to repair the damage I caused."

Miranda could hardly believe what she was hearing.

They had a pact. They were a team. How could

she do this? How could she turn on Miranda? "Does the term *breach of contract* mean anything to you? We *have* to finish it."

"I already talked with our agent about that."

Add *betrayal* to the tidal wave of feelings crashing over her head and drowning her. "You went behind my back?"

"Not in the way you think. I had to be sure that by backing out it wasn't going to hurt you. She thinks she can get them to split the contract. It would mean less money—"

"I don't care about the money," Miranda interjected.

"—and reworking what we've already written, but I know you can do it."

And how was it that Ivy knew that? Did she have a crystal ball? Had she suddenly become psychic?

"Sure," Miranda snapped back. "Don't worry about me. I'll just wave my magic wand and everything will be fixed."

Miranda knew that getting nasty wasn't going to help matters. She and Ivy had always agreed that if ever they should part ways as writing partners, they would always remain friends. But Miranda was feeling this twang of hurt in her soul, a sting of betrayal beyond anything she'd ever experienced.

And damn it, she was scared. She didn't know if she could do this on her own. And she didn't want to try.

"I know things are already complicated for you with the baby coming. I feel terrible for doing this, Miranda, I really do. We've been through so much together. But I have to. I couldn't live with myself if I didn't set things right."

That meant Miranda either had to find another writing partner or write the follow-up book from only a law perspective. With the psychological angle gone, she wasn't sure she could fill an entire book with legal advice that was unique enough to be a successful follow-up to their first book. Especially if she would be in direct competition with her soon-to-be-ex-writing partner. She didn't even have a clue where to begin.

Ivy was the creative one. The one who had taken Miranda's legal jargon and breathed life into it. Kept it from crunching on the page like dry, burnt toast.

She *needed* Ivy.

Unfortunately, Ivy was as stubborn as she was savvy. Once she made up her mind, she didn't change it. For anyone.

Too bad Miranda and Zack had completely opposite values. As a team they could probably write one hell of a book.

Miranda tamped down the panic building in her chest, the fear clawing at her insides. "Do you have the details of this new contract?"

"Our agent will be contacting us individually later this week after she irons things out with the publisher. She's doing her best to get us an extension on our deadline. Her main concern is that we'll lose our marketing budget. Or that they might choose one book over the other to publicize."

"The news just keeps getting better, doesn't it?"

"I'm *so* sorry, Miranda. I didn't plan for this. It just happened. And I want to do all that I can to make the relationship work this time."

Though she felt hurt and betrayed, she couldn't say that put in Ivy's position she wouldn't have done the same thing. One of the things they had stressed in the first book was that a woman should trust her own instincts and be tough enough, and brave enough, to take a stand for what she believed in.

How could Miranda fault her for that? Who was she to judge what was right for Ivy?

"You know," Ivy said. "If people were to find out about the pregnancy and who the father is, it could really reinforce your beliefs. You couldn't ask for a more effective publicity stunt."

She wasn't prepared to sell Zack out for the sake

of her own stalled career. She didn't have the constitution for such brutal warfare. Maybe it was silly, but she believed that what goes around comes around. And this one would surely come back to bite her in the butt.

She would find a way to make this work without taking Zack down in the process.

After listening to several more minutes of Ivy's apologies, Miranda hung up the phone feeling hurt and confused and...lonely. Barely a day passed when she and Ivy didn't speak. The idea of losing that made Miranda's stomach ache. Who would she confide in?

She didn't want things to change. She liked her life the way it had been. She was comfortable. And confident.

Suddenly, everything was different.

But sitting around feeling sorry for herself wasn't going make things better. She had a new book to plot.

Alone.

Chapter Seven

"Are you sure you know what you're doing?"

"Absolutely," Zack told his sister-in-law, Taylor. He had her on speakerphone while he unpacked the boxes in his office and she waited for her flight to board.

"Richard and I worry about you."

"Will he be home tonight?"

"He's staying in D.C. He has a dinner with some lobbyist whose name I can't recall. There are so many I lose track. You can try his cell."

He had. He'd tried both his cell and his office and he hadn't answered. "He's a busy man these days."

"Tell me about it. If he's not at work or in a meeting, there's always a charity dinner or a fundraiser we have to attend. Lately, if I get him alone for an hour on the weekend I consider myself lucky. I understand now why the other wives call themselves widows."

"He's just getting established. It will get easier." He emptied the last of the box and set it on the stack with the others. "And think how good life will be when he's elected president."

"He's determined enough. If anyone can do it, he can. And I love the way you cleverly managed to manipulate the conversation so that we're no longer discussing how concerned we are about you."

Zack grinned. Taylor knew all of his tricks. "Nothing to be concerned about."

"After everything you guys have been through, he wants you to be happy."

"I will be."

"If it gets out to the press…there's so much at stake—"

"It'll be fine." He pulled a stack of reference books from a box on the floor. He checked the subjects and set them on the appropriate shelf, alphabetically by author. "I'm already beginning to wear her down."

"I think I may have scared her. You know I always have the tendency to come on too strong."

"I'm sure she liked you," he said, grabbing yet another stack. He never realized how much reference he owned until he'd had to move it all.

"I liked her, too. I just hope she's the right one for you. You have to admit she's not the kind of woman you usually date."

In the past few months, his usual dating patterns had been the nonexistent kind. Lately it seemed as though every woman he met was just…boring. It was probably why he'd been so taken by Miranda. She didn't have a boring bone in her body. He would go so far as to say he'd never met another woman like her. "Maybe that's exactly the kind of woman I need."

"I hope so, because I get the distinct impression this one will be a handful."

So did he. That was kind of what he liked about her. She challenged him. There was never a dull moment when Miranda was around.

"She told me that you offered to throw her a baby shower. I know that couldn't have been easy for you."

"I refuse to let myself dwell on it." There was a sadness in her voice. There always was when her infertility issues came up.

"It'll happen," he said.

"I know."

He sensed a hesitation. "But...?"

"It's just that the treatment isn't exactly cheap and Richard was thinking maybe it would be best if we backed off for a couple months. Built up our savings."

"If you're having money problems you know I'm—"

"Richard would never allow it. But thanks for the offer. Besides, he's probably right. We've been at it for a solid year. Maybe we could both use a break. I've heard stories of couples going through months of fertility treatment, and when they finally give up, it happens naturally."

He hoped that was the case with Taylor. He'd been getting the feeling lately that her infertility had begun to put a strain on her and Richard's marriage. The idea made him a little nervous.

She was the best thing that could have happened to his brother. Zack had introduced them knowing they would be a perfect fit, knowing she would straighten him out. And she had.

"Rich can't wait to see the new place. Maybe we can fly in next weekend. Spend the day together?"

"That would be great." The sooner Miranda met his family, became involved in his life, the more likely she would be to want a more permanent relationship. This may not have been the way he planned his life, but all that mattered now was what was best for the baby.

"And maybe he and I can take a day to be together, just the two of us," Taylor said.

She sounded so sad. "You're sure everything is okay?"

"It's just tough, being away from him so much. Maybe I… Oh, wait, they're calling my flight. I have to go."

"Have a safe flight."

"And you have a good dinner. I'll talk to you soon."

"We will," he said, but she had already disconnected. Why did he get the feeling there was something she wasn't telling him? Something pertaining to her and Rich.

Their relationship was the model for Zack's books and seminars. He sometimes felt as if his entire career hinged on their marital success. He took comfort in the fact that Richard had just as much to lose. He was on the fast track in D.C. Someday he would be president. A divorce, for any reason, could be potential political suicide.

Besides, Zack trusted him. They had been through an awful lot together. His baby brother would never let him down.

He hoped.

* * *

It was nearly seven-thirty when Zack crossed the street to Miranda's condo. Their first official date and she'd stood him up.

He might have been worried, but when he'd peered out his front window across the cul-de-sac to her place, he'd seen her shadow in the upstairs window. Back and forth she had paced, but when he'd tried to get her by phone she hadn't answered.

He would be insulted, but to deny occasionally being so wrapped up in work that the hours slipped by unnoticed would be a lie. He didn't doubt that's what Miranda had done.

He stepped up to Miranda's porch, rang the bell and waited.

And waited.

He rang the bell a second time and waited a minute more. What was taking so long? Or had she seen him coming and was choosing not to open the door?

He hit the bell a third time, and a second later the door swung open.

There stood Miranda, a slightly dazed, marginally confused expression on her face.

When she failed to speak, he said, "Hey."

"Hey, what's up?"

"I think you forgot something."

Her brow furrowed. "Sorry?"

"You stood me up." She still looked confused, so he added, "Dinner at seven. My place."

She slapped a hand to her forehead. "Oh, my gosh! Is it seven already?"

"Twenty-five after, actually."

She swiveled around to check the clock hanging above the mantel of her fireplace. "I'm so sorry. I was working and I completely lost track of the time."

"That's what I figured. Are you ready?"

"Ready?"

Wow, she really was out of it. "To eat."

"Oh, right." She hesitated, glancing inside, then across the street to his condo.

"If you want to cancel—"

"No, of course not." She gave her head a shake. "I'm just a little distracted. I get like that when I work." She grabbed her keys and stepped onto the porch. "I'm ready."

He grinned and gestured to her feet. "You might want to lose the bunny slippers."

She looked down to the fuzzy neon-pink slippers on her feet and rolled her eyes. "Like I said. Distracted." She stepped back inside and kicked off the slippers, then slid her feet into a pair of flip-flops. "Better?"

"Much."

"Great, let's go." She shut and locked the door behind her, then walked silently beside him across the street.

"How's the writing going?" he asked as they stepped up onto the porch.

She uttered a noncommittal, "It's going."

He opened the front door for her and she stepped inside. She inhaled deeply, a dreamy look on her face. "Oh, it smells *wonderful.*"

"Everything is done. I just need to get it all on the table. You can help yourself to whatever you'd like to drink."

She followed him to the kitchen and opened the fridge. "Would you like anything?"

"A beer sounds good."

She got a bottled mineral water and a beer from the fridge while he took the lasagna and garlic bread from the oven and set it on the table with the salad, freshly ground parmesan and olives.

"I hope you don't mind that we're eating in the kitchen rather than the dining room," he said.

She shrugged. "I don't mind. I usually eat in front of the television or at my computer while I work."

He had considered setting up the dining room complete with linen napkins and candles, but he didn't want to rush things. He didn't think she was ready for an intimate, romantic meal.

He held a chair for her while she sat, then took his own seat at the opposite end of the small table.

"It looks wonderful," she said, setting her napkin in her lap.

He cut the lasagna into squares. "This won't bother your stomach?"

"I don't think so. I'm starving."

She held out her plate and he dished a piece onto it.

She looked at the plate, then at him, her brow furrowed. "I'm eating for two, remember?"

With a smile he doubled her portion then dished out his own. Before he could even get the salad served, she loaded her fork with noodles and chunky tomato sauce dripping with mozzarella and provolone cheese, blew on it for a second, then tasted.

The look on her face as she chewed was one of sheer bliss. She tasted the garlic bread next and moaned with delight. "This is amazing! Where did you learn to cook?"

"I'm a bachelor. If I didn't cook, I would starve."

She tried the salad next. "Umm! What brand dressing is this?"

"It's homemade."

"It's delicious! I'll have to borrow the recipe."

He watched her wolf down her food. Holy cow.

She was shoveling it in like a contender at a pie-eating contest. He was flattered that she was enjoying it, but after seeing her hanging over the toilet this morning, he was afraid she might make herself sick.

But what was he supposed to say? "Hey, want to save some for the rest of us?" Maybe this was the way all pregnant women ate. His experience with the maternally endowed was limited.

"Seriously," she said, taking a drink of her water. "You can't tell me you're not wealthy enough to afford a cook."

He shrugged. "Let's just say I had to do a lot of cooking when I was a kid."

"Why?" she asked bluntly.

He didn't know if he was ready to let her that deep into his head. He didn't talk about those days. He didn't even like to think about them. He'd reconciled himself with the past a long time ago.

"My mom worked," he said. It wasn't a lie. She had worked. And by dinnertime she was usually too tipsy or too tired—or a varying combination of both—to cook for Zack and his brother, and there was little money for ordering out.

"Mine was a stay-at-home mom," Miranda said, grabbing another slice of bread from the basket. "Dinner on the table every night by six-thirty. And I mean *every* night. She could be down with the flu, and she'd drag herself up out of bed to cook." She took a bite of bread and licked her lips. "Is this real butter?"

"Mixed with olive oil. Your dad didn't help out?"

"In all the years I lived there, I never saw him fix himself so much as a sandwich. As far as he was concerned cooking was woman's work. He brought home the money and my mom was his indentured slave. She did all the cooking and the cleaning and the laundry."

Which may have explained her aversion to family structure. He didn't doubt for a second that her husband had been the same way. It was common for daughters of controlling fathers to subconsciously look for the same qualities in their mate.

"Are your parents still with you?" he asked.

"Alive and kicking." She swiped up the last remnants of cheese and sauce with a corner of bread, and before she'd chewed and swallowed, was diving in for seconds. She took another wedge of lasagna and a third slice of bread.

Eating for two? Looked to him like maybe she was eating for three or four. "Is it possible you're having triplets?"

"I know, can you believe this? I'm starving! It's just so good. Maybe this means I'm over being sick."

That sounded like one of those too-good-to-be-true scenarios to him. "What does your father do?"

"My dad is a lawyer, my mom a legal secretary. That's how they met. She worked for him."

"Siblings?"

"I have two older brothers. Both lawyers."

"That's a lot of law in one family."

"Tell me about it. I was hoping to become a partner like my brothers, but because I'm female the plan was always for me to marry another lawyer, immediately begin producing offspring who would also eventually become lawyers, and give up my career to be a housewife, like my mom and my sisters-in-law. My mom wasn't allowed to go back to work until my brothers and I had moved out."

"Allowed? Are you suggesting that she didn't have a choice?"

"I *know* she didn't. It was against my father's values. He believed a mother should be home with her kids."

"And she was unhappy with that arrangement?"

"She never came right out and said so. I think she pretended to like it for my brothers' and my sakes, so we wouldn't know how miserable she was. But I could tell. Sometimes she would look at me and get this sad, almost distant look in her eyes. I think it was her way of showing me how she felt without actually saying the words."

"Somehow I can't see you playing the housewife role for anyone."

"Neither could I. My husband, on the other hand, saw things from my father's perspective. Hence my divorce."

"Why did you marry him in the first place?"

She shrugged and set her fork down. "Because it was what was expected of me. Because I was desperate to escape home and I had deluded myself into thinking things would be different for me. I thought that once we were married, Kirk would see how archaic my father's ideas really were."

"But he didn't."

"Of course not."

"In my experience working with married couples, I can't begin to count how many times I've heard the phrase, 'I thought he would change' or 'I thought things would be different after the honeymoon.'"

She took a sip of her water. "What about your parents?"

"Both deceased."

She stopped chewing long enough to shoot him a sympathetic look. "I'm sorry."

He shrugged. He would have liked to be able to say he missed his parents, or he had been devastated when they died, but the truth was he hadn't felt much of anything. When his dad passed away Zack hadn't seen him for ten years. By the time his mom died, the alcohol had eaten so much of her away, she was barely more than a shell. A ghost. "They've been gone awhile now."

"How did they die?"

He hesitated. She had been pretty open and honest with him; it was only fair he show her the same courtesy. Right? It's not as though the truth wouldn't come out eventually. "My dad was killed in a car wreck when I was in college. My mom died of cirrhosis several years ago." Because he knew she was wondering, but probably wouldn't come right out and ask, he added, "She battled alcohol addiction her whole life. The alcohol won."

"How old was she?"

"Fifty-eight."

She sat back in her seat, that familiar look of sympathy on her face. The one he saw every time he divulged the truth about his past. For some reason it was a little less condescending coming from her. It felt more genuine.

He wondered how she would react if he told her the whole truth. It's not that he was embarrassed or ashamed of where he'd come from. He simply preferred not to think about it. He'd already spent his time in therapy reconciling the past. Now people told *him* their problems and issues, not the other way around. Yet he could imagine talking to Miranda, telling her the things he'd never told anyone but his own therapist.

He trusted her. Which was unusual, since he barely knew her.

Miranda pushed her plate away, closed her eyes and swallowed deeply, as though she had a lump in her throat.

Uh-oh, she was looking a little green again.

"Everything all right?" he asked.

She took a deep breath and blew it out. "I think I may have eaten a bit too fast."

"Anything I can do?"

She shook her head, then cringed. "It'll pass. I'm sure I'll be fine in a minute."

But a minute later she looked worse. "Can I get you something else?"

Lips clamped shut, she shook her head. Her breathing sounded shallow and a sheen of sweat moistened her forehead.

"Maybe you would be more comfortable on the couch." Or from the looks of it, in the bathroom.

"If I move, it will only get worse," she said, barely moving her lips. She sat with both hands curled over the arms of her chair, her knuckles so tense they'd lost all color, as though she was holding on for dear life.

There had to be something he could do.

Before he got the chance to ask, she slapped a hand over her mouth and bolted from her seat.

Chapter Eight

"Someone kill me," Miranda moaned from Zack's bathroom floor.

Every time she thought she was feeling better, he would help her out to the couch and get her settled, then she would get that look—that wide-eyed, oh-no-not-again horror—then bolt for the bathroom.

Unfortunately, his experience with pregnant women was grossly limited. But according to his sister-in-law, whom he had phoned after Miranda's third time kneeling to the porcelain gods, it was a natural part of the process and he shouldn't worry too much. Taylor and Rich didn't have kids of their own yet, but Taylor was an aunt six times over and had dealt with her share of pregnant siblings.

She suggested that Zack be supportive without being overbearing. She also warned of mood swings and potentially erratic behavior. Miranda could be perfectly happy one minute and in the throes of an emotional meltdown the next, for no apparent reason whatsoever.

As a therapist, erratic behavior was a normal part of the job and nothing he couldn't handle. Usually. This hit a little close to home.

She sat up, steadying herself on the edge of the shower door. "I think it's safe to assume the morning sickness is still an issue."

He handed her a cool damp cloth. "Are you ready to try the couch again?"

She leaned back against the tile wall and wiped her face. "I think I'd rather go home instead."

"Are you sure?"

She nodded and set the cloth on the edge of the sink. "I just want to crawl into bed and sleep until my fourth month when *supposedly* this will all be over."

"Would you like me to stay with you for a while?"

That one earned him a very small smile. "I think I'd rather be alone. But thanks for offering."

He helped her up and gave her a second to steady

herself. The ordeal had taken a lot out of her physically. She looked beat.

She stopped at the sink to rinse her mouth, then he guided her to the door and out onto the porch. Burnt orange tinged the darkening western sky, and a chill nipped at his bare arms. A cool breeze ruffled his hair and reminded him of the brisk mornings he'd spent before dawn jogging along the shore of Lake Michigan. Lately there never seemed to be time. He'd instead used the exercise facilities in his building.

Maybe now would be a good time to take it up again.

With his hand resting lightly on her back, he walked her down the steps. He could see her fatigue in the slight dip of her shoulders, the tilt of her head. He could practically feel it radiating from inside her. Contrary to what he knew to be the truth, she looked small and fragile.

She stopped just shy of the sidewalk and looked up at him. "I can make it from here."

"We've come this far, I might as well take you the rest of the way."

"You don't have to."

"I'm here to help take care of you. Remember?"

She looked up at him as though she was about to say something. Probably that she didn't need anyone to take care of her. Then she just sighed and shook her head. "Fine."

They crossed the street at a leisurely pace. She unlocked her front door under the glow of the porch light and he preceded her inside, shutting the door behind them. The room was dark, so she switched on the lamp beside the couch.

She tossed her keys down on the coffee table and turned to him. "I had a really good time. You know, up until the icky part."

"Me, too." He genuinely enjoyed her company. Upon first meeting her, he'd been a bit uncertain of her aggressive nature. The type of woman he typically gravitated toward tended to be a bit more subdued. Yet he had—and still—found her impossible to resist. And he was sure he would get used to her constantly questioning and second-guessing him.

If nothing else, life with her would never be boring.

He gestured to the stairs. "I'll walk you up."

She glanced at the stairs, then back at him. "I feel much better."

He folded his arms across his chest. "What's your point?"

"My point is, I can handle things from here."

He didn't budge. Did she think she'd get rid of him that easily? "I don't doubt that you can."

She sighed loudly and rolled her eyes. "I'm not five. I don't need you to tuck me into bed."

She apparently *was* feeling better. The attitude was back. "Why are you so afraid to accept my help?"

She gave one of those squinty-eyed, *yeah, right* looks. "You don't really think the reverse psychology mumbo jumbo is going to work on me, do you?"

He shrugged. "Not really, but it was worth a shot."

"Look, I sympathize with your overwhelming urge to micromanage my life. It's actually sort of sweet in a warped, creepy way. And hey, I'm sure there are a lot of women out there who would love the attention. But let's face it. I'm not one of them."

"I'm allowed to worry about you."

"I'll be fine. It's not as if I don't have your phone number. Hell, I could just shout across the street and you would probably hear me. So go home. If I need you I'll call."

He sensed he was pushing her a little too close to the line and decided it would be best if he back off.

He held his hands up in surrender. "You win. I'll go."

He gestured over his shoulder to the door. "I'll lock up for you on my way out."

"Thank you. And thanks for dinner. It really was wonderful."

"My pleasure," he said, confident that there would be many more dinners together in the future.

She started to turn, and he said, "Wait."

He couldn't let her go without touching her one last time.

She sighed again, regarding him with a hint of exasperation. "What now?"

He stepped closer, his eyes locked on hers. Hers were soft and warm and intelligent. And maybe a touch bemused, as though she just wasn't sure what to make of him. In the lamplight her cheeks looked rosy and smooth and her dark hair glimmered. He had the distinct and overwhelming urge to not just tuck her into bed, but to climb in with her.

All in good time.

With one hand he gently brushed the hair back from her forehead, his fingertips barely brushing her skin, and he could swear she shivered. And, oh, man did he feel it, too. From the tips of his toes all the way to his scalp.

After a second he let his hand drop and backed away. "Give me a call tomorrow morning and let me know how you're feeling."

She swallowed, then nodded. "I promise."

For an instant he had the feeling she wanted to say something else, then she turned and headed upstairs. As he was leaving, he noticed her keys lying on the coffee table. He looked at the lock on her door, then back to the keys and grinned to himself.

He scooped them up and walked out.

Miranda woke slowly, the muted sound of music penetrating the haze of sleep clouding her head. Who would be playing music that loud this late at night?

She peeked through partially open lids at the clock and realized it wasn't last night anymore. It was morning. A brand-new day. Another day to be sick.

She could barely contain her excitement.

The music stopped and she heard voices, and what sounded like a news program. Had she left the television on last night before she went to bed?

As she gradually came awake and the cobwebs cleared, she remembered that she had gone to Zack's last night, had come home and gone straight to bed. She hadn't even turned on the television. Could her neighbors be playing their television loud?

The harder she listened, she could tell the sound was coming from downstairs in her own condo. There was only one person she knew who would have the nerve to pop over and let himself in uninvited.

She sat up and swung her feet to the floor, regretting the sudden movement the instant her stomach went haywire. If she had learned anything these past couple of weeks it was no sudden, jerky movements first thing in the morning.

She sat very still for a minute, until the woozy feeling in her belly and the swimmy sensation in her head reached a tolerable level.

Still in her jammies, she walked very slowly down the hall. She passed her office and was reminded of Ivy's phone call yesterday, and the way she had paced the floor for hours struggling to brainstorm new ideas for a book. And coming up blank.

She shook the thought away. One problem at a time.

She found the source of her current dilemma sitting on her couch, watching the morning news, dressed in a T-shirt, nylon shorts and running shoes. His disguise, the baseball cap and sunglasses were beside him on the cushion. He was sweaty, rumpled and unshaven, and she couldn't stop herself from wondering how a man so sophisticated and cultured could look so…hot. And the worst part was, she preferred this look to the serious guru persona.

If she wasn't so nauseous she would be in some serious trouble.

She propped her hands on her hips and went for a stern look. "Do we have a listening problem?"

He looked up at her and flashed that mischievous grin—the one that was beginning to look awfully familiar—and her attraction shimmied up a level. She felt herself melt the tiniest bit more. She never would have imagined the guru would have a cute, playful side to his personality, but there it was, smacking her right in the face. And for a second she forgot all about being sick, and instead began to imagine what he looked like under that T-shirt.

Yep, she was in serious trouble.

He grabbed the remote and switched the television off. "Good morning."

She adopted a tone to match the look. "Don't 'good morning' me. What are you doing here?"

The smile never wavered. "Watching television."

For a smart person, it was amazing how well he played dumb. "Do I even want to know how you got into my house?"

"I used the key."

Of course. That made perfect sense.

If she disregarded the fact that she hadn't given him a key. "And how exactly did you come into possession of a key to my condo?"

"Last night I told you I would lock up. I couldn't very well lock the dead bolt without a key. So I borrowed yours."

The man had a logical answer for everything, didn't he? "And let me guess. Now you're just returning them."

Again with the adorable grin. She had to struggle not to smile back.

"You're cute when you're pretending to look angry," he said.

She raised her chin a notch. She hated the way he could see right through her. "Who says I'm pretending?"

He rose from the couch, still wearing that grin, distracting her with the flex and play of all that lean muscle and golden skin. For a another second she forgot all about her upset stomach. She was too busy inspecting his biceps. The weight of his thighs.

Very nice.

He gestured to the recliner. "Have a seat and I'll get your breakfast."

"Breakfast?" This visit involved food? Dinner last night, and now this?

"Tea and crackers, right?"

"But—"

"Sit," he said sternly, and was en route to the kitchen before she could produce a snappy comeback.

She huffed out an impatient breath. Who did he

think he was, barging into her house and ordering her around?

She should follow him. She should get indignant and make a big fuss about him smothering her. She should rant and complain until he promised to do things her way.

The thing was, having her breakfast prepared and served to her was a tough one to resist. When was the last time she let someone pamper her a little? Not to mention that despite just dragging herself out of bed, she was exhausted. Putting up a fuss, starting an argument, sounded like too much darned work right now.

Would it kill her to let it slide this *one* time? Just so long as this never happened again. Later, when she was feeling up to it, they would have another chat about boundaries.

And where his began.

She shuffled to her recliner and settled in.

"When it's a good time for you, I'd like to get together and coordinate our schedules," he called from the other room.

"I cleared my schedule so I would have time to write," she called back. "My life is not what you would call exciting right now."

"Then I'll just give you a copy of mine. I don't want to be halfway across the country when you have a doctor's appointment."

She could hear the clink of flatware against stoneware, the crinkle of the cracker package. "My four-month checkup is on Monday the tenth. Does that work for you?"

"That's perfect. I leave for Washington that Tuesday."

But that was barely three weeks away. He just got here!

Wait a minute, was that disappointment she was feeling? Sure she liked Zack, but she didn't need him around.

She kept her tone casual and asked, "How long will you be gone?"

Zack reappeared with her tea and crackers. "Why, are going to miss me?"

She made a show of rolling her eyes at him. "Don't flatter yourself. I'm just trying to coordinate our schedules."

"Fourteen days, ten appearances."

Yow. "Tight schedule, huh?"

"It always is. And it's exhausting."

He handed her the cup and set the plate beside her on the table, then made himself comfortable on the couch.

"Thanks." She sipped and of course it was perfect. Perfect strength, just the right amount of honey. How did he *do* that? He'd been here less than twenty-four hours and already he knew the exact way to prepare her tea?

"I guess you're not feeling too bad today," he said.

She set her cup down. "What makes you think that?"

"The snark. When you feel okay all I get is attitude. When you feel sick you get kinda soft and mushy." He leaned forward slightly, that come-hither look in his eyes. "I like it when you're soft and mushy."

Suddenly she *was* feeling a little soft and mushy, mostly in her head.

She distracted herself with nibbling the corner of a saltine. "I don't feel too bad, actually. Queasy, but nothing like last night."

"I'm glad."

She was, too, because she had a long day ahead of her. She'd called her agent yesterday, and news from the publisher was expected today. She was hoping and praying they gave her some idea of what they might be looking for. Some inkling of a direction she should take. On her own she was clueless.

Zack laced his fingers behind his head and leaned back against the cushion, and she was instantly distracted from her thoughts. She was instead hypnotized by the flex and pull of muscle in his arms, the corded strength in his neck. She could swear he was doing it on purpose. Was he trying to make her drool down the front of her pajamas?

There was a quick knock, then the front door flew open.

"Hey, Miranda! Are you—"

Chapter Nine

"Decent?" Lianne stopped dead in her tracks when she saw Miranda and Zack sitting there. "Oops, sorry! I didn't know you had company."

It didn't escape Miranda that Zack's disguise was inconveniently on the couch beside him. But it would be rude not to formally introduce them.

"Lianne, this is Zack," Miranda said, avoiding last names. Lianne had been on the self-help roller coaster enough times to recognize the name Zack Jameson. "Zack, this is my neighbor, Lianne."

Zack rose to his feet. "We met yesterday."

Lianne looked at him, a confused little smile on

her face, as though she was sure she'd seen him somewhere before but she couldn't quite place it. As a writer, she was incredibly observant. It was probably only a matter of time before recognition set in.

It didn't take long.

Lianne's mouth fell open and she uttered a breathy, "Oh, my God." She looked from Zack to Miranda, then back to Zack. Their secret was definitely out.

And it had been such a good morning up until now. Wasn't this going to be fun to explain.

"Zack, could you give us a minute?" Miranda asked.

Zack grabbed his cap and glasses and put them on. "Sure. I still have unpacking to do. It was nice seeing you again, Lianne."

"You, too," Lianne said.

"We'll talk later," Zack told Miranda, then let himself out.

The second the door snapped closed Lianne turned to Miranda and asked, "Have you completely lost your mind?"

She never had been one to mince words. Miranda sighed and let her head fall back against the chair. "I think so."

"How in the hell did you wind up sleeping with…" Lianne jabbed an accusing finger her way. "The radio show! That's when it happened, isn't it?"

"Well, we weren't actually on the radio when it happened."

"I knew it! I knew you were acting weird when you got back. For two weeks before the show all you could talk about was what a cretin this guy was, then you came back and…nothing. When I asked you what he was like you just shrugged it off." She was in full rant, now. "You told me the guy was from Chicago."

"He is from Chicago."

"When you said Chicago I figured you actually slept with him *in* Chicago."

And what difference did it make where she slept with him? Had it been Chicago instead, she wouldn't be any less pregnant. It was done. There was no going back. "Does it really matter where it happened?"

"I suppose not." Calmer, she sat on the couch and folded her legs under her. "So let me see if I have this right. You have no plans to marry him, or even be in a committed relationship with him?"

"Nope."

"You're going to have a child outside of marriage with the family-values guy?"

"Yup."

"What did you do? Ask yourself, 'of all the men in the world, who would be the worst possible one to father my child?' then have sex with him?"

She made it sound as though Miranda had slept with the hunchback of Notre Dame. "Jeez, Lianne, he's not *that* bad."

"Of course he's not. He's smart and rich and ranks way above average on the looks scale. But, correct me if I'm wrong, don't you two have a slight conflict of interest?"

"I didn't plan this, you know. It just sort of happened."

"And he's okay with not getting married?"

"He wants to, but I told him no."

"Of course you did."

"I would really appreciate it if you didn't say anything to anyone about this. You can probably imagine what a mess that would potentially be."

"Of course I won't. But damn, Miranda, if you knew he was moving in across the street you could have at least warned me."

Miranda bit her lip.

A smile crept across Lianne's face. "You had no idea, did you?"

"I knew he was temporarily moving to Texas. The across-the-street part was a surprise."

Lianne shook her head. "Oh, man, am I glad I'm not in your shoes. A man like that, there's no doubt he's going to try to convince you to marry him."

"So?"

"We've already established his many assets. Any woman would be ecstatic to marry him."

"Any woman but me, I guess."

"Admit it, you like him."

To claim otherwise would be a lie. "Okay, I like him."

"And since you slept with him once, I'm assuming the idea of sleeping with him again is not completely revolting."

Far from it. "Of course not. But I still don't see the problem."

"So what you've got is a gorgeous, rich, man whom you admittedly like and want to sleep with, living across the street and who is determined to win you over."

When she said it that way… "What's your point?" she asked, no longer sounding as sure of herself.

"My point is, if you're going to get through this a single woman, you have to find the strength to keep telling him no."

"I'm not going to make it to the party," Miranda told her mom, across the safety of the phone line, where she wouldn't see the look of disappointment on her face. She'd been dreading this call all week, knowing it would buy her a one-way ticket on the Reed family guilt trip.

Of course, attending her niece's birthday party would have been twice as bad.

From the kitchen she heard the whistle of the kettle, the clatter of dishes, as Zack fixed her tea.

"We haven't seen you in months," her mom said. "You promised to be there."

It wasn't the first time she'd broken a promise. She'd have thought they would have come to expect it by now. Hadn't her life always been one gigantic disappointment to them?

"But I'm sick," Miranda told her. "It's an awful flu. Joey and Todd would never forgive me if I passed it along to their families."

She didn't say it, but Miranda knew what her mom was thinking. There was always a logical reason, a rational excuse for Miranda to miss out on every family function for the past six months.

This time it was at least partially true. She did feel sick, although it was unlikely she would be passing it on to someone else. And even though she wasn't showing yet, in fact she had actually lost weight in the past month, she was afraid her mom and sisters-in-law would take one look at her and be able to tell. They would know she was pregnant, and Miranda still hadn't decided what she wanted to tell them. And the longer she waited, the harder it would be.

"Is everything okay with you?" her mom asked. "Other than the flu, I mean."

It was the perfect opportunity to blurt it out, to tell her the truth. But she couldn't make herself do it. Not yet. "Everything is fine. Why wouldn't it be?"

"You've been so distant."

Could she blame her? Miranda's book hadn't exactly been well received by her family. The constant chiding, the man-hater jabs from her flawless sisters-in-law, were not Miranda's idea of fun.

"I've just been busy working on the second book," she told her mom. A blatant lie. She hadn't written a word. Heck, she hadn't even come up with a viable idea.

"Maybe you could come by for dinner next week. We miss you."

Zack appeared in the kitchen doorway with her tea and crackers. He looked at her questioningly, as though he was unsure if he should interrupt her conversation. She motioned him into the room.

"I'll call you," she told her mom. She missed them, too. She had always been close to her family. But things change. "I have to go now."

"Take care of yourself, and call me when you're feeling better."

"I will. Talk to you soon." She hit the disconnect button and dropped the phone in her lap. Zack set her tea and crackers down on the table beside her. She wondered how much of the conversation he'd heard. And he knew better than to ask. Her relationship with her family was one of their don't-even-go-there subjects.

"You know, if you gave me a key, you wouldn't have to get up and open the door for me every morning," he said. "Instead of sitting here waiting for me to fix it, you could be having breakfast in bed."

"Not happening." She'd grudgingly opened the door for him every day for the past two weeks. She had accepted the fact that when it came to him taking care of her, he wouldn't accept no for an answer. And though she would never go so far as to admit it to him, she was grateful for his help.

But there was still that annoying little voice in her subconscious, whispering warnings in her ear, telling her she'd begun to grow dependent on him.

In the other ear she could hear Lianne snickering, telling her that if she didn't take control, didn't start laying down some rules, she was as good as married already.

It was sound advice, but she couldn't dredge up the energy to do a damned thing about it. She would worry about setting things straight when she was feeling less sick, and not so tired all the time. She felt like such a slug lately. She barely made it through lunch every day without falling asleep in her plate. It was the sort of fatigue that seemed to settle deep in her bones and suck every last bit of energy from her muscles.

And if she was going to be perfectly honest with herself, she would have to admit that she liked Zack. *Liked* as in, she was beginning to form a major crush on the guy.

He was so different from the men she was used to. So damned agreeable. And though she would like to be able to say she had control in their relationship, he definitely had the upper hand. The weird thing was, he never took advantage of it. If he was pushing too far, and saw her beginning to squirm, he didn't hesitate to back off. Although lately she'd been doing a lot less squirming and he'd been insinuating himself a little further into her life every day.

But instead of feeling smothered and claustrophobic it was almost…comfortable.

Zack took a seat on the couch, where he always sat. As usual, he was in his jogging attire, his hair adorably mussed from a combination of sweat and the baseball cap on the seat beside him.

His facial hair was fuller and shaped into a neatly trimmed mustache and goatee. And so far no one had recognized him—no one but Lianne—so apparently the disguise was a success. The real test would be today at her doctor's appointment.

"What time is your appointment?" he asked, as though he'd plucked the thought right out of her mind.

That seemed to be happening a lot lately. To both of them. She would say something and he would claim to have just been thinking the same thing. And the more time they spent together, the more it occurred. It was as though they had some weird psychic connection.

She'd heard of couples having similar experiences, but technically they weren't a couple. Could the pregnancy be to blame? Could having a baby together link two people that deeply?

And if so, would it go away after the baby was born? Or would they be stuck reading each other's minds for the rest of their lives?

"I have to be there at four," she told him. "We should leave at three forty-five."

"We'll take the Mustang." It wasn't an offer so much as a demand.

She would normally interpret that sort of comment as pigheaded and sexist. Especially coming from him. He was the man, so he should do the driving. But having lived across the street from him for two full weeks now, she knew his desire to drive had nothing to do with gender, and everything to do with the vehicle.

That car was his baby.

More than once, in the throes of agonizing, unbearable writer's block, she'd watched him from her office window pampering it. She'd witnessed him rubbing the body with a buffing cloth until the shine was bright enough to induce a migraine. She had seen him lift the hood for no other reason than to stand and gaze lovingly at the engine. He checked the tire pressure each time he drove it, before and after the trip.

She would go so far as to say that he was obsessed.

Her brothers had been the same way with their adolescent muscle cars, but now they preferred their foreign imports. Mercedes or BMWs. She knew her sisters-in-law would settle for no less. Those two were the ideal trophy wives, plucked out of identical shells, who had given birth to the perfect offspring. Visiting their homes was like taking a trip to Stepford.

Or hell.

Which is why she rarely visited.

"Do you think you'll feel up to visiting with Taylor and Rich on Saturday?" Zack asked.

She would force herself. Rich was flying in all the way from D.C. to meet her, and from what

Miranda understood, he'd had to cancel several speaking engagements just to find the time.

"I'm sure I'll be fine."

"Will you be all right if I head home?" Zack asked. "I have a column I need to finish."

"Of course," she said, but there was an undeniable hint of disappointment tugging at the edge of her conscience.

He usually stayed longer, at least until she'd finished her breakfast. He washed the dishes for her and set them on the drain board to dry—a task her ex would have never lowered himself to perform. By then, if she was still feeling icky, Zack would sit and talk with her until her stomach settled and she had the energy to haul herself into the bathroom for a shower.

That little voice gnawed relentlessly at her ear, telling her she was getting too close. Too dependent. She'd lost control.

She would definitely have to do something about this. When she felt up to it, that is. Besides, what harm would one more day do? She was sure she would be feeling better tomorrow. She would talk to him then.

And maybe tomorrow she would come up with a damned idea for the book. Maybe then she would start writing and everything would be okay.

That familiar feeling of dread curdled in her stomach like sour milk. The feeling she got every time she let herself think about how productive the past week hadn't been.

Zack's brow wrinkled. "Everything okay?"

"Sure, of course."

"For a second there you were looking a little green."

That's funny, she was feeling a little green, too. "I'm fine, really. I don't feel too bad this morning. Go ahead and get to work."

He looked hesitant. "You're sure?"

"Don't I sound sure?" she snapped.

He shrugged. "No need to bite my head off."

Relax, Miranda, it's not his fault. He's not the one ruining your career. You're doing that all by yourself. She couldn't help thinking about her ex and what he would have done in a situation like this. Suffice it to say he would still be berating her for raising her voice to him.

Zack, on the other hand, shrugged it off.

Was he for real? Or was it an act? Would his true personality eventually emerge?

"Sorry," she said. "I'm okay. And I know where you are if I need you."

"I'll call in a bit to check up on you." He stood and put on his disguise. "Call if you need anything."

"I will."

He opened the door, then hesitated. "Are you sure you're okay?"

No. Not really. Right now everything was a mess and she didn't have a clue how to fix it.

She forced a smile. "Really, I'm fine. I think I'm just sick of feeling sick."

"It'll get easier," he assured her. "Just give it some time."

She hoped he was right, but for some reason she feared this was only the tip of the iceberg, and before they got better, things were going to get a lot worse.

Zack called to check on her an hour after he left. Then again an hour later. He called again at three to confirm that they were meeting in his driveway at three-forty to leave for her appointment. If nothing else, the guy was thorough.

At three-forty as planned, she stepped out onto her porch and, as promised, Zack was waiting for her, standing beside his baby.

She grinned, shook her head and started across the street. At this time of day she didn't worry too much about the neighbors seeing since most of them were still at work. Besides, sooner or later they were going to catch on. And when her pregnancy began to show, which would be soon, there would be no disguising what role Zack played in her life. That didn't mean they had to know who he was.

According to Lianne, there had been some talk. Who was the elusive new neighbor, and why was he always going to Miranda's house? Lianne had smoothed it over by telling one of their neighbors that Zack was a friend of Miranda's who had been looking for a place to live and coincidentally there had been one right across the street.

It would be only a matter of days before the information made the rounds. And the best part was, it wasn't a lie. Not completely anyway.

She crossed the street. The Mustang glimmered in the sunlight and Zack stood there like a proud father, beaming.

"Men and their toys," she said.

"Toy? This is a Mustang Boss 429."

"Really. Well, it's…cute," she said, but only because she knew it would irritate him.

He looked horrified and appalled. "Did you just say *cute?*"

"Yeah."

"This car has a 335 horsepower engine. It has F60x15 raised white lettered tires, Magnum 500 wheels, a trunk mounted battery, competition suspension, slotted and drilled disc brakes and traction lock rear. This is a muscle car, sweetheart. It is not cute."

She held her hands up in surrender. "I stand corrected. It sounds fun."

That one earned her another squinty-eyed glare.

"Sorry. How about, it sounds exhilarating and… inspiring?"

"Better."

"Can I drive it?"

He looked a little surprised by the question. "You want to drive?"

"If it's that awesome an experience." She held out her hand for the keys. "Sure."

"Right now?"

Maybe he thought she didn't know how. He'd never actually seen her drive. She hadn't been away from the complex for weeks. When she needed something and even talked about taking a quick trip to the corner store, he always offered to run up and grab it for her. And since she never really felt up to doing it herself, and she knew he was looking for opportunities to take his baby out, she acquiesced. "Why not? I do know how."

He shot her a scrutinizing look. "You think you can handle all this power?"

She shot him a look right back. There were still a lot of things he didn't know about her. "Don't be fooled by the soft, feminine exterior. I had older brothers. They taught me to drive in cars like this."

He shrugged and held out keys. "Knock yourself out."

She couldn't suppress a smile. He would actually let her drive it. His baby. That had to be some kind of progress. Right? Some sort of sign.

"That's okay. You can drive."

He looked thoroughly confused.

"I didn't really want to drive," she explained. "I just wondered if you'd let me."

"So that was a test?"

"Sort of, I guess."

Grinning and shaking his head, he walked around to the passenger's side and opened her door for her. She slipped into the polished leather bucket seat. The interior was pristine.

He braced his arm on the top and leaned into the open doorway. "If this was a test, how'd I do?"

"You passed with flying colors."

He stood there for a moment, bent over, his eyes pinned on hers. They were deep and swimming with an emotion she just couldn't read. It wasn't desire exactly, but something like it. Lust maybe, but subtler.

Whatever it was, the hair on the back of her neck shivered to attention and her heart fluttered. Then he leaned forward the tiniest bit, his mouth so close, his lips looking soft and tasty.

And she wanted a nibble.

His eyes strayed to her mouth and settled there. Oh, boy, he was going to kiss her. She felt herself moving, leaning closer to the temptation of his mouth, to what she knew would be as fantastic an experience as it had been before. She wanted to taste him and touch him.

He was going to kiss her and there was nothing she could do to stop him.

He hovered there for a second, while her heart went wild in her chest, then he just smiled and shut her door.

In those few seconds, she was so breathless she felt as if she'd run a marathon. It took her a second to realize what had happened, what his intention had been.

He had been testing her, too. He wanted to know what would happen if he'd tried to kiss her. And by leaning toward him, she'd answered loud and clear.

What if the next time he didn't stop?

Chapter Ten

Zack's disguise was a big hit at the doctor's office. He was a nameless face that no one spared more than a courteous nod or smile.

He'd been in the public eye long enough to know the tricks of blending in. Not only was it the baseball cap, glasses and beard, or the casual jeans, nerdy button-up short-sleeved shirt and tennis shoes. It was the manner in which he carried himself. Body language that made him appear slightly less sure of himself.

It was the hint of hesitation when he entered a room. The subtle hunch of his shoulders under the

shirt that was just a tad too large. The barely per-
ceptible dip of his head when people made eye
contact. He was wary, and maybe a little shy. A
loner. Definitely not the kind of man you would
expect to find up on a stage lecturing in a crowded
auditorium or promoting his latest book on the
morning news show.

He was no different from everyone else in the wall-
to-wall-packed waiting room—and, holy cow, he'd
never seen so many pregnant women in one place.

After several minutes of sitting there in ano-
nymity, Miranda leaned close and whispered, "I
have to admit I was a little worried about us being
discovered, but, damn, you're good. I feel as though
I'm sitting here with a stranger."

"Years of practice," he whispered back. It was
the only way he could have a relatively normal life.
Otherwise the media would constantly hound him.

When Miranda was called into the examining
room soon after, the nurse looked at Zack a little
curiously when he didn't take off his sunglasses.
But he had a ready-made excuse for that, too.

"I'm sensitive to fluorescent light," he told her.
"Gives me migraines."

She clucked sympathetically, suggested he try
taking melatonin, then took Miranda's blood pressure. After she'd asked a couple dozen questions,

she handed Miranda a paper drape. "Everything off from the waist down."

Oh, boy. He'd never anticipated her having to take her clothes off. And judging by Miranda's expression, neither had she. "I thought this was just a tummy check."

"Your pap came back irregular. He wants to recheck it, just in case."

Zack's heart took a dive. What did that mean? Was she sick? Did she have *cancer?* Was the baby in danger?

"Irregular?" he asked. "Should we be concerned?"

"It's just a precaution," the nurse assured him.

Miranda shrugged it off. "I've had this before and it always turns out to be nothing."

The nurse scooped the chart up and headed for the door. "The doctor will be in shortly."

When she was gone, Miranda looked at the drape, then to Zack. "I didn't realize there would be a pelvic."

"Does my being here make you uncomfortable? If so I can sit in the waiting room."

"Does it make *you* uncomfortable?"

Maybe a little, but he didn't want to leave. "I'm in it for the long haul. If I can't handle a pelvic exam, I'll be useless in the delivery room."

"True," she agreed. "Besides, it's nothing you've never seen before, right?"

"That is one way to look at it."

"And since I don't plan to give birth with my clothes on, eventually you're going to see me at least partially naked."

"I can wait in the hall while you undress," he offered.

"That's silly. We're both adults. I think I can trust you to just turn around." She squinted her eyes at him. "I can, right?"

He grinned. "Of course."

He turned toward the sink to give her privacy. He heard the sound of clothes rustling and the crinkle of the paper drape.

"Uh-oh, I'm turning around," he teased.

"Hilarious," she mumbled, but he could hear a smile in her voice. Then he heard her gasp.

"Everything okay?" he asked.

"Table's cold." There was a bit more rustling and shifting, then she said, "Finished."

He turned back around. She sat at the edge of the table, covered from the waist down. Her jeans and panties lay in a heap on the chair beside the door.

This was the closest he'd had her to naked in three months. With any luck, he wouldn't have to wait until December to get her out of her pants again.

She took a long, deep breath and blew it out.

"Feeling okay?" he asked.

"Not sick, if that's what you mean. This is just a little weird. Having you here makes it feel more… real, I guess."

He was about to ask her what she meant—after weeks of morning sickness how could it *not* feel real—but the door opened and the doctor stepped in the room.

He introduced himself to Zack, then looked over the chart and asked a few questions of his own. Zack asked about the abnormal pap again, just to be sure.

"It's just something we need to keep an eye on. If there are abnormal cells, they would likely be expelled during the birth. In any case, it poses no harm to the fetus. Now," he said, "let's see how things are progressing."

Zack stood at the head of the table and witnessed his very first pelvic exam. He wasn't sure what he expected, and was surprised by how quickly it was over.

The external segment of the program came next. The doctor pressed down on Miranda's belly, palpating, he called it, to measure the growth of her uterus. "Looks good. A little high for a first pregnancy."

"What does that mean?"

He made a notation on her chart. "It could mean nothing. Would you like to feel it?"

Miranda nodded enthusiastically, and following his lead, pressing down on her own belly. Her brow knit with concentration, then her face lit and she gasped, "Oh my gosh! I feel it!" She looked up at Zack, eyes bright with excitement. "You have to feel this!"

The doctor showed him where to press, but Zack was a little concerned by how far he had to push, the pressure he was using. What if he hurt her?

"I don't feel anything," he said.

"Push harder," Miranda urged.

He did as she asked, cringing on the inside.

Then he felt it. A surprisingly small, solid lump just below her navel.

She looked up at him and smiled. "Feel it now?"

"I do." He wasn't sure what he'd expected a uterus to feel like. In fact, he couldn't remember ever wondering. But there it was. He was touching it. His baby, *their* child, was in there.

It was hard to imagine something so little would eventually fit a seven- or eight-pound human being.

Amazing.

"Now let's hear that heartbeat," the doctor said.

Miranda looked up at Zack and smiled. "This is my favorite part."

He pulled out what Zack was guessing to be a fetal heart monitor. He smeared some clear goo on it and pressed it to her stomach. It took a second or two of sliding the monitor from one side to the other, then he heard a steady, surprisingly fast, thump-thump-thump.

It was faint at first, then louder and stronger.

That was *his* baby's heartbeat. His and Miranda's.

A tidal wave of emotions crashed down over him and threatened to suck him completely under. Pride and joy and awe. And fear.

Until she gave his hand a squeeze, Zack hadn't even realized she was clutching it. And he suddenly understood what she meant about the pregnancy not seeming real. In that instant it had become truly real to him, too. A tangible living, breathing human being. He'd actually touched it, felt it growing inside her, heard its little heart beating.

Pretty soon her belly would be full and round with their child. *Their* child. A little girl or boy. Would it look like him, or be the spitting image of Miranda?

For several seconds his own heart seemed as though it was working its way up his throat.

He thought he had accepted that she was pregnant, that he would be a father. All along he'd *known* they were having a baby, but now he really felt it.

He *knew* it.

The night he and Miranda spent together took on an entirely new significance. It had never been just sex to him. He knew they had connected. He'd just never understood, never comprehended, how deeply. They had done something amazing that night. They had created a life. And that little person deserved everything Zack never had. It was his responsibility to see that it happened.

He was more determined than ever to convince Miranda that they should be a family.

"You can get dressed," the doctor told her. "We'll schedule the ultrasound for your twentieth week."

Zack kept her hand wrapped in his until the doctor left the room. And even then he didn't want to let go. He wanted to keep touching her. He wanted to be close to her. It ate away at him, a gnawing ache in the pit of his stomach.

It wouldn't be the first time in his life that he wanted something that was unattainable. Something just out of reach. But eventually he would get what he wanted.

With persistence and patience, he always did.

As they left the room, she reached out and

clasped his hand again, and held on while she checked out and made her follow-up appointment.

They walked out to the car hand in hand. He opened her door, waited until she was buckled in, then walked around and got in. As soon as the car was in gear she was reaching for him again, twining her fingers through his.

He wasn't sure what had prompted this sudden need to touch, but he sure as hell wasn't complaining. It felt as though she'd opened a door, propelled them that much closer to the altar.

"Wasn't that amazing?" She wore a half smile on her face, and her free hand rested across her stomach.

"Yeah, it was."

She looked over at him, cheeks rosy, eyes bright. Man, she was pretty. "Being here with you, it feels so right."

If that wasn't the understatement of the millennia. "Yes, it does."

She sighed and rested her head back, her thumb grazing absently back and forth across the side of his palm. More than a tickle, but not quite a stroke. And her perfume, had she always smelled this good? Warm and sexy and maybe a little on the wild side.

Her skin felt soft and warm, her hand small but sturdy. He glanced over at her. She looked content.

She looked happy.

And he felt…

Oh, man, he was getting aroused. Sparks of desire popped and crackled, igniting in his blood, and her touch worked like a soft breeze to fan the flames.

What was wrong with him? It had been years since holding hands with a girl was enough to make him hot. Maybe high school or, hell, probably more like junior high. Sure, he was attracted to Miranda, but he wasn't a kid. There was a time and a place, and right now wasn't it.

It had to be all of the touching they'd been doing today, or her hormones acting like an aphrodisiac.

"I feel as though something changed while we were in there. I don't even know how to describe it." She gave his hand a light squeeze, shimmied in her seat so they weren't sitting so far apart. "I feel like we're closer somehow."

No kidding. Any closer and she would be sitting in his lap. Thank God for the gearshift.

"Like we bonded emotionally," she continued. "Does that make sense?"

"I think so." There was something undeniably depraved about the fact that for her this was some sort of sweet, tender moment, and he had a hard-on.

And she kept up with that slow stroking, uttering occasional, breathy sighs.

Damn, she was killing him.

He was so distracted he nearly blew through a red light and had to slam on the brakes to stop. And only when the car behind him honked did he notice it had turned green.

"You okay?" she asked.

"Fine," he lied. How the hell could he be expected to concentrate on the road when all the blood in his body had drained into his groin?

By the time he aimed the car down their street, he felt as though he was on the verge of crawling out of his own skin. But, damn it, it wasn't his fault. She was the one who kept touching him. The one talking about being closer. The one generating enough pheromones to take an entire football team to its knees.

He couldn't have asked for a better time to make his move, but for some reason it felt dishonest. As though he would be taking advantage of her. He would sleep with her when he knew she was good and ready. And not a minute before.

It was his duty, his obligation, to protect her. Even if that meant protecting her from himself.

He pulled into his driveway and cut the engine, eager to escape. He got out and walked around to open her door, and before she could get a hold of him, he pocketed both hands.

It was pretty sad when a grown man couldn't hold a woman's hand without getting into trouble.

Miranda got out of the car and looked at his hands, wedged deeply in his jeans pockets. "Is something wrong?"

"Nope." Nothing a cold shower wouldn't cure. "So, I guess I'll see you later."

Confusion tucked into the crease just above her nose. "You're not going to walk me home?"

Any other day and she would be insisting to walk herself across the street. After all, she didn't need anyone to take care of her. She wrestled bears and ate nails for breakfast.

She picked a hell of a day to break that charming tradition.

He glanced wistfully at his condo. "Uh, yeah, sure."

They walked side by side and crossed the street to her porch. He waited with one foot on the porch, one on the steps, while she rummaged through her purse for her keys and unlocked the door. "Would you like to come in?"

Yes.

No.

Damn it.

"I don't think so. I'd better get home."

"Are you sure?" For the first time, in all the time

he'd known her, she looked unsure of herself. Afraid even.

He didn't like it.

"Next time," he told her.

She dropped her keys and purse just inside the door. "What's wrong, Zack?"

"Nothing is wrong," he said, but he could see that she didn't believe him. "I'm just...tired."

Lame Zack. Very lame.

"You're lying. You never pass up an opportunity to come over and take care of me. Today I figured I would have to beat you back with a stick."

If she kept looking at him that way, her eyes soft and confused, her cheeks flush, she would need that stick.

"I want to know what happened," she insisted. "Why you got so tense and uncomfortable on the ride home. What did I do?"

Jeez, she was persistent. "It's nothing, okay? You didn't do anything. Everything is fine."

She reached up, touched his arm just below his elbow. He felt as though she'd zapped him with a live electrical wire.

He couldn't help it; he flinched.

He could see the color drain from her cheeks like sand through a funnel. She took a step back, toward the door, almost as though she were afraid of him.

This was a Miranda he'd never met. An insecure, apprehensive Miranda. "The appointment. It was too much, wasn't it? That's why you won't talk about it. You changed your mind."

"Miranda, what are you talking about? Changed my mind about what?"

"Me, the baby. You don't want us anymore."

Chapter Eleven

Is that what Miranda thought was happening here?

He couldn't win. If he got too close, she pushed him back, and when he stepped back, she thought he was abandoning her.

This must be the erratic behavior Taylor had warned him about. He wished he could find some happy medium, a clear-cut set of rules to follow. But he had the sinking feeling there were no rules. He was flying solo and blind. He was knee-deep in doo-doo with no boots or a shovel. Or was it a paddle?

"You can tell me the truth," she said. "I can take it."

No, she couldn't. He could see her lower lip already beginning to quiver. She was a wreck. He may not have known Miranda well, but one thing he did know was that she wasn't a crier. She was tougher than that. This had to be one of those maternal mood swings. Estrogen overload.

Cars were pulling into driveways up and down the street. People were arriving home from work. The last thing they needed was an audience.

He gestured to the door. "Let's go inside and talk."

She nodded, tears hovering just inside her lids. He could see that she was trying like hell to hold them back.

When they were inside, he shut the door behind him. And since Lianne had been known to drop by unannounced, most times without bothering to knock, he flipped the lock, too. He took off his sunglasses so Miranda could see his eyes, see that he was sincere. Now, if he could just get her to stop looking at her own feet.

"Miranda, look at me."

She very reluctantly lifted her chin, gazed up at him with huge, grief-stricken eyes.

"I did not change my mind."

If he'd been thinking his words would fix things, that it would calm her down, he was wrong. Instead the tears spilled over and rolled down her cheeks.

She sniffled and wiped them away. "Then why were you being so quiet? Why did you jump when I touched you? Do I disgust you that much?"

Disgust him? Where was she getting this? He wanted to tell her she was being ridiculous. And irrational. But somehow he doubted that would help.

How had he gotten himself into this mess?

Since reasoning with her no longer appeared to be a viable option, he did the only thing he could do. He pulled her into his arms and held her instead. She was so freaked out she was actually trembling. "You *do not* disgust me. Quite the opposite. Which was why I didn't want to come over."

She clung, her arms around him, hands fisted in his shirt, one teary check pressed to his chest. "I don't understand."

He cupped her chin and angled it up so he could see her face. Her nose was red, eyes bloodshot, the color in her cheeks uneven and splotchy. Some women looked good when they cried. Sort of soft and delicate.

Miranda wasn't one of them.

When she cried, she looked as though she really meant it.

He wanted to kiss away her tears, could almost taste the salty dampness on his tongue. He wanted to wrap his arms around her and hold her until she stopped trembling.

He just plain wanted her.

He sighed and shook his head. "Miranda, I'm doing my best to be a gentleman, but you're sure as hell not making it easy."

Confusion creased her forehead. "But you are a gentleman."

Was he going to have to spell it out for her?

"I'm a guy. And I'm attracted to you. When you touch me, I get turned on. Even if we're just holding hands."

Her response was a soft, breathy little, *"Oh."*

"I want you, Miranda. But I can't do this halfway. Either we're together or we're not."

She was quiet for several seconds, her lip clamped between her teeth. "So, what you're saying is, you're not touching me because you want to?"

He wiped the remnant of a tear from her cheek with his thumb. "As backward and irrational as that sounds, yes. That's exactly what I'm saying."

He could see her processing that. "So, you not touching me is, what, for my own safety?"

"You could say that, yeah."

"So if I did this…" She turned her face into his hand and—aw, hell—brushed her lips across the pad of his thumb.

Her breath felt warm, her lips soft and damp. Where the hell was that cold shower?

She looked up at him. "That would be bad, right?"

"That's not funny."

"I'm asking for informational purposes only. I mean, I don't want to accidentally do something that might set you off and put me in danger."

"In that case, yes, it would be bad."

"In *that* case, I guess I really shouldn't do this." She flattened her hands on his chest, slid them slowly upward, wrapped red-tipped fingers around the back of his neck. Her body felt warm and soft pressed against him. And just like that, the spare room in his jeans disappeared. He fisted his hands at his sides, gritted his teeth.

He wanted to push her away, needed to, but the message was getting scrambled somewhere between his brain and his arms. He wanted to be the good guy, but he could only take so much. If she kept toying with him, he would crack.

She stroked the sides of his throat. Her nails lightly scratched his skin, nearly driving him out of his mind. He bit off the groan working its way up from his chest and summoned the last shred of self-control.

This was the Miranda he recognized. The one

who knew exactly what she wanted and wasn't afraid to go after it.

"Keep it up and you'll be sorry," he told her.

She flashed him one of those sexy, seductive smiles. "I'm counting on it."

It was fascinating to watch, the gradual and inevitable deterioration of a man's self-control. Especially in a man like Zack. A man who *never* lost control.

It was a thrilling sensation of power she'd never experienced before. Heady and intoxicating. Euphoric even.

She wanted to press her lips to his. She wanted to know how he would taste. What his beard would feel like against her chin.

He watched her through eyes heavy with desire, waited, balancing precariously on the outermost edge of his fortitude. All it would take was one little push, one nudge, and they would be lovers. They would be, in his eyes, a couple. One step closer to a door she was terrified to venture through. And she knew without a doubt that if she let this happen there would be no turning back. Everything would change.

Was she ready for that?

"I want this Zack. I want this more than I've ever

wanted anything in my life. But I'm not ready to make any promises." She touched his face, stroked the bristly hair along his jaw.

"I want it, too, Miranda. I do." Slowly, reluctantly, he backed away, and she let her hands fall to her sides. "But I can't. Not this way. For me it's all or nothing."

"I'm not ready."

He wedged his hands in the pockets of his jeans. "Then we wait."

And she respected him for that. She really did. They had made some real progress today.

So why was it beginning to feel as though, for every step they took forward, they inevitably took one backward? Until they were right back to where they started.

Miranda was finally going to meet Zack's brother.

Rich and Taylor's flight had landed twenty minutes ago, so they would be appearing any minute now. She and Zack waited in baggage claim, and the longer they stood there, the more Miranda got to thinking, what if Rich didn't like her? Wasn't he the ultimate spokesman for Zack's program? What if, unlike Taylor, he didn't approve of Miranda and Zack's relationship?

A month ago it wouldn't have mattered. Miranda wouldn't have cared what anyone thought. But things were different now. She knew how close Zack and his brother were, and that wasn't a dynamic she wanted to mess with.

"Relax. He's going to love you," Zack said.

Miranda shot him a look. One that said, Why should I care?

"You're chewing your lip. You only do that when you're nervous."

Did she? Figures he would notice that sort of thing.

"Okay," she conceded. "I might be a little nervous."

He tugged her to him, her back to his chest. He wore his disguise, and didn't seem all that worried about people recognizing them. He looped his arms around her waist and rested his chin on the top of her head. She relaxed against him, felt herself being enveloped by the warmth of his skin, the strength of his arms. She liked when he touched her this way. It made her feel so…normal. Like they were an actual couple.

"Don't worry. We're going to have a great weekend," he said.

She hoped so.

"There they are!" He let go of her, and for an

instant she thought that maybe he didn't want Rich to see them looking so intimate. Then he took her hand, weaving his fingers through hers, and tugged her along beside him.

It took Miranda a minute to pick Taylor out from the crowd, and when her eyes landed on Rich, she sucked in a surprised breath.

In shorts, a polo shirt, a baseball cap and sunglasses, he looked so ordinary. Likewise, Taylor was dressed casually and had pulled her hair back in a ponytail.

Where was the power couple Miranda had been expecting? They seemed so average.

But before Miranda could give it much more thought, Taylor threw her arms around her and hugged her. She was so stunned, she almost forgot to hug her back.

"It's so good to see you again!" She held Miranda at arm's length and looked her up and down. "You look wonderful! How have you been feeling?"

"Better," Miranda told her. She was feeling queasy right now, but not that overwhelming sense that if she moved she would hurl. And it was only eight in the morning.

Rich and Zack embraced, and not one of those standoffish, I-love-you-but-let's-not-overdo-it deals that men do. They grabbed hold and held on, really squeezed, like they meant it. It was obvious they had a very special bond.

Miranda had never seen her brothers hug this way. In fact, she wasn't sure if they had *ever* hugged each other.

"Rich," Zack said. "I'd like you to meet Miranda. Miranda, this is my brother, Rich."

He had a smile just like Zack's, and when he took his sunglasses off and hooked them in the vee of his collar, she could see that it extended all the way to his eyes. They were the same brilliant blue as his brother's and just as warm and congenial.

They hadn't exchanged a word yet and already she liked him.

But what would he think of her?

He clasped her hand between his two and shook it warmly. "I've heard so much about you, I feel as though I already know you."

And he was nothing like she expected. "I'm almost afraid to ask what you've heard."

He laughed. "All good, believe me. Although for the life of me I can't imagine what you're doing with this idiot." He pointed a thumb toward his brother.

"Thanks," Zack said, giving him a playful punch in the arm. "Let's get the bags."

They located the turnstile and grabbed the luggage and golf gear from the conveyer belt. As they walked out to the rented SUV, Miranda quietly watched the interaction between the three of them. The camaraderie. Taylor was definitely one of them. She was family. Zack and Rich were brothers in every sense of the word. They weren't just family. They were friends.

She couldn't remember a time when she and her brothers had been so openly affectionate. And they didn't seem to like her all that much. Mostly they treated her as though she was beneath them. A nuisance they tolerated only because they had to. With her sisters-in-law she was coolly polite.

Even her marriage had lacked that element of warmth. The closeness. Kirk never would have grabbed her hand and held it, laced his fingers through hers the way Zack did as they were walking to the car. He wouldn't have brushed his fingers against her arm as he helped her into the passenger seat, or smiled that easy smile that said he was happy to be with her.

She was the black sheep of her family. The outsider. Even with her own husband. And it wasn't anyone's fault but her own. She had settled for that. She'd let it happen. The next time she settled down with someone, whether that someone happened to be Zack or another man, things would be different.

From the airport they went straight to the Dallas Zoo. She might have thought a couple like Taylor and Richard would prefer a museum tour. Another reminder that she'd drawn too many conclusions, and that she had the artistic ability of a gnat.

From the zoo they went to the aquarium, then on to dinner at a casual, authentic Mexican restaurant. The mood was light, festive and Miranda couldn't remember the last time she'd had so much fun. Nights out with Kirk had always been more of an obligation than a pleasure. If they weren't accompanying an important client to the theater or the opera they were at a fund-raiser or out to dinner with a business associate. They never did anything just because it was fun.

They had a long leisurely meal, chatted about current events and movies and politics. Rich was conservative but not too far to the right, passionate without being preachy or judgmental. Miranda was a staunch Democrat, but after only one day she could see herself voting for a man like Rich. There was something about him, something so honest and trustworthy.

And then there was Zack. All through dinner he sat close, his arm draped casually over the back of the booth behind Miranda, absently grazing her shoulder with his thumb. All day they had held hands, touched in the intimate little ways couples often did. No one would guess they weren't a real couple. And Miranda was having a tough time trying to figure out what it was that was holding her back.

Later, at Zack's condo, they drank wine—or in Miranda's case, mineral water—and just talked. Zack and Rich had endless funny stories, anecdotes from their childhood and college. Although, Miranda noticed, neither said much about their parents. Maybe some things were better left unsaid.

It was after midnight when Rich and Taylor turned in and Zack walked Miranda across the street to her condo. The air was warm and thick, but a light breeze blew.

"I had a really good time today," she told him. "Rich is great."

He took her keys and opened the door for her. He was in the shadow of the porch light, but she could just make out the shape of his face, the contour of his features. "He told me that if I don't marry you, I'm an even bigger idiot than he thought."

"What did you tell him?"

"That I'm working on it."

Something struck her just then. The honesty of his words maybe, or the good vibes from the day, but on impulse she rose up on her toes and kissed him. It was meant to be brief, not much more than a peck, but Zack caught her behind the neck and held her there, deepening the kiss.

And she melted. Her knees went soft and her head felt light. He tasted like wine and something spicy.

He curled his fingers into her hair, slipped his other arm around her and drew her against him. The perfect end to a perfect day. But now she didn't want it to end. One step back and they would be in her living room. And only another couple dozen to the bedroom.

"Come inside," she whispered against his lips. "Stay with me."

She felt his hesitation. He leaned back to look in her eyes. "Marry me."

It was so tempting, the idea of saying yes, if for no other reason that to get him in her bed. But she could never do that to him. She could never be that dishonest.

And he knew her answer; she could feel the pull of his disappointment before she even spoke.

And still she wasn't ready to throw in the towel. "I'm not saying no."

He let go and backed away and she knew she'd lost him. "It's not the same thing."

No, it wasn't. But even after today—especially after today—she couldn't make any rash decisions. She was compromised by the warm fuzzies. What if she said yes tonight and woke in the morning to realize she'd made a mistake? It wasn't a decision she could just take back. "I'm just not ready."

"Then I can't stay." He stepped back, away from her, even farther out of the light, but his disappointment was as tangible and solid as the concrete under her feet. As intense as her own. Yet she respected his decision. She even admired him for it. But there had to be some middle ground in their values. Some sort of compromise.

"We tee off at nine-fifteen tomorrow," he said.

"I'll be ready."

"Then I guess I'll see you tomorrow."

"I guess."

He hesitated, like he might say something else, then he turned and headed across the street.

Regret and uncertainty ate a hole in her belly as she watched him go. Watched him open his own door and disappear inside.

Today, for the first time in her life, she'd felt as though she was part of a real family. One that would never judge or belittle her. One that would treat her as an equal. She felt like she belonged. She hadn't realized until today just now how much she longed for that. How important it was to her. And it made her all the more determined to take this slow. To be sure it was what they both really wanted.

He was perfect in every way, still it felt as though something was missing, as if they were both holding something back.

And until she figured out what that something was, things would have to stay just the way they were.

The condo was still and silent when Zack walked through the door, but as his eyes adjusted to the dark, he saw Rich sitting on the couch, a glass of wine balanced in one palm. "I thought you went to bed."

He swirled the wine, then sipped. "And I thought I wouldn't see you until morning."

Answering a question with a question. Not a good sign. On the outside, Rich seemed fine. His marriage, his career. But Zack knew his brother well enough to recognize when something was wrong. Today, something had been off.

Zack settled into the chair across from him. "You want to tell me what's going on?"

"I can't hide anything from you, can I?" Rich sighed, a long tired sound. "Money. Infertility. Take your pick."

"Is that it?"

"That's not enough?" He shook his head. "But you know Taylor. She's a trooper. Every time we get bad news, or she has another miscarriage, she picks herself up, brushes off and forges ahead."

"I could recommend a counselor—"

"We're fine, Zack. If I feel my marriage is in danger, you'll be the first one to know."

Zack hoped that was true. And Rich couldn't fault him for worrying. They depended on each other. Riding the coattails of Zack's reputation, Rich had built the foundation for his career in politics. Traditional family values. Parading their infertility issues in the media hadn't been easy for either of them, but it had been good for the cause. In the long run it would pay off.

Zack in turn reaped the benefits. Because of Rich and Taylor he'd built his empire. Although sometimes he felt as if they'd built a house of cards. One wrong move and it could all come crashing down.

"She's the right one for you," Rich said.

It took Zack a second to realize he was talking about Miranda. "I know."

"If it wasn't for the baby, would you have pursued her? If you didn't have to worry about the media and protecting your reputation?"

There wasn't a doubt in his mind. "Absolutely."

"Remember that."

"Why?"

Rich set his empty glass on the coffee table and pulled himself to his feet. "Just remember. Don't forget what's really important. Don't be so busy living by the rules that you forget to live."

That made no sense. If they didn't live by the rules, didn't have standards, life would be chaos.

Rich started to walk toward the stairs, then stopped and turned back to him. "Do you think if Mom and Dad had divorced sooner, if he hadn't cheated and lied, things might have been different for us?"

It wasn't often Rich mentioned their parents. They had determined a long time ago that things were what they were, and there was no point dwelling on it. Eventually the wounds would heal, the scars would fade.

Zack shrugged. "Maybe. Maybe not. We'll never know."

Rich nodded. "I guess not. See you in the morning."

Zack watched him walk up the stairs, heard his footsteps overhead as he walked to the bedroom, wondering what that was all about.

He also had the uneasy feeling there was something going on that Rich wasn't telling him.

* * *

The following day was as packed with activity as the last. Golfing, shopping, sightseeing. By 7:00 p.m., when they dropped Taylor and Rich at the airport, Miranda was exhausted. The fact that'd she'd hardly slept the night before wasn't helping matters. She dozed most of the way home from the airport and Zack had to nudge her awake.

"Home sweet home," he said.

She opened her eyes and realized they were in her driveway. Usually he parked in his and walked her across the street. She covered a yawn with the back of her hand. "Can't wait to get rid of me, huh?"

"I leave in the morning. I have a few things to pick up, and packing to do."

Two weeks away from each other. It seemed like such a long time. "It's going to be strange, you not being here."

"I think the time away might be good for us." He put the car in Park and looked over at her. "It'll give us both the chance to figure out our feelings. To step back and decide where we go from here."

What he was really saying was, he wanted her to make a decision. Not that she blamed him. He was probably tired of being strung along, the prospect of a relationship being dangled in front of him like bait. And honestly, she didn't know if two *years* would be long enough to sort all the muddled emotions, the fears and expectations tangled up inside her. And maybe he was right. Maybe they did need to step back.

"I think that's a good idea," she agreed.

"If there's an emergency, you can reach me through my publicist."

In other words, "Don't call me, I'll call you." A little harsh. But fair.

"And if you need anything in the house, you have the key. Or the Mustang. Drive it all you like."

She was so used to having Zack around, talking to him every day. She could hardly imagine what it would feel like with him no longer there. And that scared the hell out of her.

"So, I guess I'll see you in two weeks," he said.

She needed to say something, do something, but for the life of her, she didn't know what. So instead she got out of the car. Resisting the almost unbearable urge to call him back, to run after him, she watched him back out and drive away.

They were doing the right thing, yet she couldn't shake the feeling that she had just royally screwed up.

Chapter Twelve

This stepping-back thing they were doing sucked lemons. Whoever coined the phrase "Absence makes the heart grow fonder" must have had a crystal-ball link into Miranda's head.

The past fourteen days had been the longest, most lonely, of Miranda's entire life. Without Zack, something was missing. She felt homesick. Which made no sense at all since she was home.

Maybe home just wasn't the same without him there. Had she really become so attached to him? So used to him being around?

You'll get over it, she kept telling herself. This

feeling will go away. But every day it just got worse. And even stranger, she didn't want it to go away. It may have scared her half to death, but at the same time, something about it felt good. It felt right.

She considered all the sacrificing he'd done for her. The compromise. He'd moved clear across the country, resorted to wearing a disguise so they could be left in peace. He'd taken care of her when she was sick. Cooked for her. Given her keys to his house and his car.

What had she done? Other than act as a slow cooker to his offspring. And what if, after all this time to think, he'd decided she wasn't worth the trouble? Too high maintenance—that's what her ex used to say. What if Zack came to the conclusion that a relationship with her was just too damned much work?

The idea made her sick to her stomach, which a week ago wouldn't have meant much, but she hadn't had a bout of morning sickness in six days. It was anticipation throwing her out of whack now.

Zack was due home any minute. She knew because she'd checked the airline Web site to confirm that his flight had landed on time. She'd checked twice, just to be sure.

Okay, three times.

If he was even on the plane. What if he had changed his plans and decided to go back to Chicago instead?

He wouldn't do that, she assured herself. He said he would be back, and he would. He wouldn't leave without talking to her.

She fought the urge to sit at the front window and watch for him, to listen for the throaty growl of his car approaching. Instead, she busied herself dusting, picking up clutter, straightening the rug by the front door. And, oh, look, the curtain in the front window looked crooked. She definitely needed to fix that.

"Would you sit down already?" Lianne said from her perch on the couch, glancing up from her computer screen. "You're making me nervous."

A case of writer's block had her setting up a temporary office in Miranda's living room. Also, Miranda suspected, Lianne just liked to see her in agony.

So agonized, she hadn't been sleeping well. She'd risen at the crack of dawn this morning. Early enough to catch Lianne sneaking the elusive "new boyfriend" she'd been seeing for the past month out the door. The "new boyfriend" Lianne had already dated, married and divorced. Twice. The one who lived in the complex around the corner.

In one fell swoop, Lianne had broken every

single documented dating rule. But, in her current situation, Miranda didn't think she had any business lecturing anyone on relationships.

Hell, maybe she never had.

Miranda toyed with the silky drape, pretending her eyes weren't wandering toward Zack's empty driveway, then down the street. "I like a clean house, is that a crime?"

"I think I liked you better when you were sick. When all you did is lie around and moan."

"I did not!"

Lianne grinned. "Chill, honey. He'll get here when he gets here."

Was she that transparent? That obvious?

She feigned innocence. "I have no idea what you're talking about."

Lianne rolled her eyes. "Uh-huh. Whatever you say."

Miranda blew out an exasperated breath. Lianne was right. She was acting like an adolescent with a crush. "All right. I'm waiting for him. Are you happy?"

Lianne snorted out a laugh. "Why don't you just give the guy what he wants?"

A commitment. An exclusive relationship. Just thinking it made her heart flip-flop in her chest.

"What are you waiting for? A sign from God?

That man is the closest thing to perfect for you that you're ever likely to find. When will you learn to trust him?"

Because trusting Zack wasn't the problem. The person she was having trouble trusting was herself. Which was even worse.

Zack was too good, too perfect for her in almost every way. So naturally there had to be a catch. There had to be something there that she wasn't seeing. But Lianne, the unwavering optimist, would never understand Miranda's convoluted logic.

Miranda didn't even understand it.

At least she no longer had to worry that marrying Zack would ruin her writing career. She was doing a thorough job of that all by herself. In two weeks, when she was expected to hand in the outline for the book she had supposedly been hard at work plotting, it would officially be over. And oddly enough, she didn't really care anymore. For now she wanted to concentrate on being a good mom. And maybe someday down the road, a halfway decent wife. She could go back to being a lawyer.

From outside she heard the deep growl of a car engine approaching. There was only one car in the cul-de-sac with a rumble like that.

Her heart jumped up into her throat and her knees turned into soggy noodles.

She saw a brief flash of black from the street and darted away from the window, pressing her back to the wall beside it. If he looked over she didn't want him to see her standing there. She didn't want him to know she'd been watching for him.

"Why don't you go talk to him?" Lianne said.

"I can't." If she ran across the street and threw herself into his arms—and that's exactly what she was afraid she would end up doing—the balance of power would shift to his side of the court. She had to keep up the illusion that she was in control.

"You're impossible." Lianne snapped her laptop shut. "At least Zack has the good sense to come over and work things out."

"What do you mean?"

"I mean he's on his way across the street."

Now?

Already?

Didn't he need to go inside first? Unpack? Take a shower?

Did this mean he missed her so much he couldn't wait to see her, or he couldn't wait to break it off so he could get on with his life?

Her hands felt numb and shaky and a peculiar buzzing hummed in her ears. Two minutes ago she could hardly wait to see him, now she was terrified. "You had better not be screwing with me, Lianne."

She gestured to the window. "Look for yourself."

"If he really is walking across the street, I don't want him to see me watching him."

"There is something seriously wrong with you." Lianne rose from the couch and tucked her computer under her arm. "Someday you're going to look back on this and realize how ridiculous you're acting."

Maybe. She hoped so.

The bell sounded, reverberating through her skin, into muscle and bone. The ring in her ears became a clang, and she felt so dizzy and light-headed she had to grab the side of the couch for support.

If it was anyone but Zack, Lianne was dead meat.

"Well?" Lianne said when Miranda didn't move.

She couldn't move. Her legs felt heavy, as though they'd been weighted down with lead, then cemented to the carpet.

"Don't worry, I'll get it." Lianne walked to the door and flung it open.

There was a short pause, then Miranda heard Zack say, "Oh. Hi."

"Don't worry," Lianne said. "I'm on my way out."

That feeling of heaviness, the tingly numbness, was creeping up into her arms.

The door closed behind Lianne—slammed actually—then it was Zack standing there. Zack, who she had desperately missed for fourteen days. Zack, clean shaven and sexy as hell in faded jeans, docksiders and a T-shirt.

His hands were wedged in his pants pockets. "Hi."

She swallowed the monster-size lump in her throat, but her voice still came out scratchy and uneven. "Hi."

"I missed you."

His honesty stunned her. Didn't he realize that he was giving her the upper hand? Giving her all the control? Maybe he knew and just didn't care.

Once again he'd managed to do exactly the right thing.

He took a step toward her. Then another. Then one more, until he was standing right in front of her.

She sucked in a deep breath, gathering her courage. *Say what you're feeling you idiot. Go out on a limb and trust your feelings.*

"I want us to be a couple," she said, the words tumbling out before she could edit them for content. "An exclusive, committed couple."

Maybe she hadn't meant to be *that* honest, but his grin made it worth the effort.

"Do you really mean that, or are you just trying to get into my pants?"

"I really mean it."

He cupped her face in his hands and brushed his lips over hers. So tender and sweet. And rather than feeling freaked out and claustrophobic, she felt... happy. But what if he asked her to marry him? Commitment she could do, the holy bonds of matrimony might be pushing it a bit.

But he didn't ask. Instead he nibbled her lower lip, sank his fingers through her hair. "At least ten times a day I had to fight not to pick up the phone and call you."

"Me, too," she admitted. That tingly numbness had moved into her head, buzzed around in her brain. "No more stepping back."

"Agreed." He deepened the kiss, and the space around them seemed to spark and sizzle with desire. She always knew they had good chemistry, but this was off the charts.

Rather than walking her to her bedroom, he swept her right up off her feet and carried her there. She did a mental once-over of her bedroom. Were there any dirty underwear on the floor? Were the sheets clean? No embarrassing feminine products lying out in plain sight?

No. Yes. No.

They were in business.

She nibbled his neck, ran her fingers through his hair. She wanted to touch him all over.

He set her down beside the bed, kissed her until her head felt mushy and her knees were weak. She tugged his T-shirt from the waist of his pants and broke away only long enough to pull it over his head. He did the same to her, then went to work on her shorts. There was a sense of urgency, as though they were in a race to see how fast they could get each other naked.

He laid her down on the bed and eased in beside her. No matter what she did, how she touched him, it wasn't enough. She couldn't get close enough. She wanted to curl up inside of him.

That night in the hotel had been hot and erotic. There had been a sense of urgency. Of danger. Now they had all the time in the world. If they wanted to make love all night, into the wee hours of the morning, then sleep until noon, there was nothing to stop them. No eleven-o'clock checkout. No flight to catch.

No awkward goodbyes.

Tonight she didn't want to rush. She just wanted to lie there and enjoy.

His hands stroked and explored, moved over her body like an erotic dance, teeth nipped at her skin. She let herself sink deeper under his spell. Let the warm shivers settle in deep and take hold, until the shivers became a quake. A rumble of sensation and emotion that rocked her from head to toe, from the inside out, then back in again.

She tried to open her eyes, but they felt weighted down and lazy. She was neither asleep nor awake. Caught somewhere between dream and reality. He was talking to her, sexy words that seemed to blend together and muddle up in her brain until they sounded like nonsense.

More. She needed more. She needed it now.

She felt like unreeling herself across the mattress, stretching as far as her muscles and tendons would allow. Lengthening her bones. But when she tried, the width of his hips got in her way. So instead, she wrapped her legs around him, drawing him closer. Felt his hard length against the part of her that was aching and needy. She crossed her ankles and locked herself around his hips, trapping him.

A groan rumbled from Zack's chest and his lips came down hard on hers. Demanding and sweet at the same time. Aggressive and determined but undeniably gentle.

The room spun around her like a carnival ride. She felt that if she didn't feel him inside her right this instant, she would go out of her mind. And because he could read her thoughts, anticipate her every want and need, he rocked his hips just so, eased himself inside her with one long, slow, stroke.

Yes…

She let him take the lead, set the pace. She gave herself permission to let go and trust him, convinced with every fiber of her being that no two people had ever been closer, had ever connected so completely, as she and Zack did at that very moment. And when she heard him moan low in his chest, felt his muscles tighten and coil, she lost it. Instantly and completely. Her own strangled moan was all she could hear, all she could comprehend, as the pleasure crashed down and dragged her under. Excruciating and perfect.

And for the first time in a long time she wasn't afraid.

Miranda lay in bed, limp and sated after some very enthusiastic morning sex.

"Are you still with me?"

She opened one eye. Zack lay on his side next to her, propped up on his elbow, looking down at her with that grin. The adorable, vaguely mischievous one that told her he was up to no good. "Sort of."

"I thought I was the one who was supposed to roll over and go to sleep."

"What can I say? You wore me out. What time is it anyway?"

He glanced over at the digital clock on her bedside table. "Seven-thirty."

"Ugh. Too early." She closed her eyes. "Need sleep."

"Wake up." He nibbled her throat, her chin, the shell of her ear.

She groaned and pulled the pillow over her head. He'd kept her up until well after midnight, which lately was way past her bedtime.

They hadn't discussed the possibility of him spending the night. All she knew was that she'd drifted off to sleep in his arms, and when she'd opened her eyes, the room was flooded with light and there he lay beside her. It didn't feel as weird as she thought it might. In fact, she kind of liked it. It felt…right.

He tried to tug the pillow away, but she held on. "Are you going back to sleep?"

"Gee, you think?" she mumbled.

"Give me another ten minutes." She felt a very large, warm hand cup her left breast. Pinch lightly. "Twenty tops."

"I'm tired," she protested. "I'm sleeping for two."

"I'll make it worth your while. I promise."

She knew that was a promise he would keep. She couldn't be one hundred percent positive, but she was pretty sure that pregnant sex was different from regular sex. It felt more passionate. More intense. But it wasn't enough to keep her conscious.

She heard him talking but she was already drifting off. Into a deep, dreamless sleep.

When she opened her eyes again she was alone, but there was a note on the pillow beside her.

Went home to work.
XOXO
Z

She pressed the pillow to her nose, inhaled the scent of Zack on it.

Nice.

She rolled over and looked at the clock. It was already after ten. She collapsed onto her back and sighed. She'd slept for almost nine hours—give or take—and still she was exhausted. But if she didn't get up now, she would probably sleep all day. And she should at least make an attempt at writing. Maybe a night of sin and debauchery was exactly what she needed to get the creative juices flowing.

She shoved herself out of bed and stumbled, eyes half-closed, to the bathroom. Twenty minutes later, freshly showered and dressed, with her hair pulled back in a ponytail, she headed down the stairs to the kitchen.

She foraged through the fridge, found a slice of leftover pizza and scarfed it down. Lately, in the past week anyway, it seemed as though all she did was think about food. Even her misery hadn't been enough to crush her voracious appetite.

Next she polished off the leftover chow mien Lianne had brought over for lunch yesterday, then rounded the meal off with a handful of chocolate-covered pretzels.

After she ate, she brushed her teeth, applied her cherry-flavored lip gloss and a touch of mascara, then headed down the hall to her office. She stopped in the doorway.

Just go in, she urged herself. *You can do it. Today is the day you'll be brilliant. Just one quick, painless step.*

Anyday now her agent would be calling and nagging, warning her to get the proposal in the mail pronto. But she couldn't do it. She couldn't take that first step, because she knew when she did, when she took her seat and booted her computer, her mind would still be as blank as a recently scrubbed chalkboard. The ideas, the answers, just weren't there.

Swallowing back the dread clawing its way up her throat, she headed down the stairs instead. She grabbed her keys from the coffee table and headed across the street.

She considered knocking, but figured they were past that formality. It was unlocked, so she let herself in. The condo was quiet and still, but she caught the scent of something spicy and delicious drifting from the kitchen. Despite having just scarfed half the contents of her refrigerator, her stomach rumbled in anticipation.

Zack was nowhere to be found on the first floor, so she went upstairs. She found him in his office, at his computer tapping away on the keyboard, brow wrinkled with concentration.

Whatever he was doing, he was utterly immersed. For a minute she stood there undetected, watching him. Memorizing the contours of his face, the shape of his lips and eyes. The way his head cocked slightly to the left when he was focused. She had always been drawn to attractive men. Although in her experience, many were lacking the corresponding personality.

Zack had looks, personality, intelligence. He was honest, and he had a great sense of humor. And he was amazing in bed. What more could she ask for? When she figured that out, she would probably be racing to the altar.

He looked up, saw her standing there, and his face spread wide with that happy-to-see-you smile. "Good morning."

"Um, it's afternoon actually."

He looked at the clock. "So it is. I guess the time got away from me. Did you sleep well?"

"Like the dead." She took a tentative step over the threshold. "Am I disturbing you?"

"Nope. I was just finishing up next week's column."

An undeniable and intense sting of jealousy snapped through her. If only she could write like that. If only she knew where to begin.

"Give me two minutes and I'll be finished."

"No rush."

She'd only been in his office a few times for short periods. She'd never really taken the time to investigate. You could tell a lot about a man by the contents of his office. It was very masculine. Dark maple furniture, forest-green walls. And clean. Not just clean, but organized. As perfect as the rest of the house.

Too perfect, maybe?

She rolled her eyes. Don't even start, she chastised herself. She kept her house clean, too, and she was as flawed and quirky as the next person.

Probably worse.

She wandered across the room to the bookshelf, scanning the titles neatly lined there. Mostly psych reference. A few books on finance. The shelf below it was devoted entirely to past issues of various car magazines. Pretty run-of-the-mill. Men always kept the interesting stuff hidden. A lesson she'd learned the hard way.

Several years ago she dated a very conservative middle-school teacher she'd met through a mutual friend. He was acutely normal. Average to the point of being boring. And at the time, that was exactly what she'd been looking for. At that point in her life, she didn't want any surprises. Just easy and predictable.

So what if they didn't exactly burn up the sheets? He was nice and he was polite and didn't have any strange hang-ups. Or so she thought. Until she used his computer to check her e-mail one morning while he was in the shower. He wouldn't mind, she figured. What could he possibly have to hide?

On the desktop she noticed a drive named "fun stuff," and naturally she figured it was where he kept his computer games. Maybe a joke or two. So, being the curious type, she opened it.

No games or jokes. What she found was file after file of Internet porn. Which in itself wasn't a terrible thing. Men liked to look at naked women. No big deal. The problem was, as she began opening the files, there were no women. Apparently the reason their sex life wasn't exactly smokin' was because she wasn't an adolescent male.

She turned to Zack. "I have a question."

He looked up at her. "Okay."

"Hypothetically, if I were to ask if I could do a system-wide search of your computer, would you let me?"

He sat back in his chair, calmly folded his hands in his lap and looked at her as though she had sprouted a second head. "Huh?"

"You heard me."

"You think I'm a Soviet spy or something?"

She felt a dash of disappointment. "So the answer is no?"

"This is another one of those tests, isn't it?" He sighed and pushed his chair back, then gestured to his computer. "I'm not sure what you're expecting to find, but have at it."

Maybe he was bluffing. She stepped closer to the side of his desk, as if she might just do it. He didn't flinch. "You would really let me look?"

"I'm not going to let you look." He clasped a hand around her wrist and tugged her down into his lap. "I'm going to *make* you look."

"It's okay. I believe you. Really." She tried to pull herself up, but he hooked an arm around her waist so she couldn't get away. She was instantly struck with an overwhelming sense of peace, a feeling of safety. He would always take care of her, be there for her.

It wasn't an illusion. It was real.

And if she kept doubting him, he was bound to get tired of trying to prove himself to her. The day would come when he would look at her and think, She is so not worth it.

His chest molded against her back, solid and dependable. And warm. Almost steamy.

Hmm, this was nice.

With his free hand he manipulated the mouse and opened a "search" window. "What are we looking for? Government secrets…dirty pictures?"

She bit her lip.

He glanced up at her, a grin tugging at the corner of his mouth. "It's dirty pictures, isn't it? Or are you looking for evidence of illicit chat room discussions? Video clips involving small mammals?"

"You've made your point," she said, but didn't make an effort to untangle herself from his grip.

"Have I?"

"No more tests?"

"You promise?"

"I promise."

He loosened his arm, but kept it looped around her. "For the record, I don't haunt chat rooms or surf the Web for porn. I'm not going to deny having purchased a magazine or two at some point in my life. But even if I was the kind of man who got off on Internet porn, considering my professional image, do you really think I would be stupid enough to keep the evidence on my computer?"

She'd never really thought of it that way.

He shifted her in his lap, so he could see her face. "Next time if you want to know something, just ask."

"I will. I promise."

A book on his desk caught her eye. Tucked away, under a stack of manila folders, was the binding of what looked like a photo album.

She was instantly intrigued.

She reached over and tugged the corner. "Family pictures?"

"A few."

"Do you mind if I take a look?"

He shrugged. "Help yourself."

She pulled the album from under the folders, struck with an undeniable shiver of excitement.

He watched over her shoulder as she flipped it open. The first few pages were filled with older photos, from when he and his brother were kids. They could have been plucked directly from the set of *The Brady Bunch*. "Groovy clothes."

"What can I say, it was the seventies."

There was a shot of Zack and Rich with their father. The photo was taken outside, in the woods. They stood close, heads bowed, examining some small item their father was holding. "Your dad was a handsome man. You look just like him."

He flashed her a grin. "So, you think I'm handsome?"

She rolled her eyes. "Oh, please. Men who look as good as you always know how good they look."

She flipped the page to a five-by-seven shot of his family. Zack couldn't have been more than ten or eleven. It was your average, run-of-the-mill family portrait.

Until she looked closer.

The smiles were a little forced and didn't quite reach their eyes. His mom was young and strikingly beautiful, yet there was something about her, her eyes maybe, that looked old and tired. And sad. "Your parents were a handsome couple."

"You've heard the saying 'Looks aren't everything'?"

She heard a hint of sadness in his voice. "She drank a lot?"

"Every chance she got, until she drank herself to death."

Her heart ached for Zack and his brother. But seeing no need to dwell on it, to kill his good mood with crummy memories of his past, she flipped the page. She was propelled forward in time about ten years, into the mideighties, to a photo of a hard-core heavy-metal rock band in what looked like a garage studio.

It took a second to process that the lead singer, the one with the long, teased hair, skintight red leather pants and leopard print shirt, was incredibly familiar. "Is this *you?*"

"You could call these my rebellious days."

"You were in a hair band? And, oh, my God, is that an *earring?*"

"I wanted to be a rock star."

She leaned forward to get a better look. "Oh, my gosh, Zack, you were hot!"

He grinned. "We were actually pretty good."

"The keyboard player looks like, oh, my God, is that Taylor?"

"She looks different with pink hair, huh?"

"Is that how you two met?"

He nodded.

The rest of the pages were empty. And just when it was getting good. She shouldered away a dash of disappointment and closed the album. She wanted to see more. Know more. "I feel so inadequate. I was a total nerd in high school."

He shot her a disbelieving look.

"No, seriously, I was. All I cared about was getting good grades. I was under the delusion that it would make my father proud. Wasn't I surprised when I realized all he really wanted me to do was get married and make babies."

"But you didn't have children with your husband."

"I wasn't ready." She leaned back against his chest, let her head rest in the crook of his neck. This was comfortable. This was very comfortable. "I wanted to focus on my career. The honest truth is, I wasn't ready to get married, either."

"So why did you?"

"He was the son of my father's business partner. As long as I can remember they talked about us getting married. After years of hearing how perfect someone is for you, I guess you get brainwashed into thinking it's true."

"So it was an arranged marriage?"

"Archaic as that sounds, I guess in a way it was. It goes back to that need to please my father. What I didn't realize at the time is that I was actually marrying my father. Kirk was just like him. He wanted a wife to raise his children, have dinner on the table every night and throw dinner parties for clients. He didn't just *want* me to. It was expected. It was never about what *I* wanted."

"Did your husband physically abuse you?"

His question nearly knocked her off his lap. She raised her head and looked up at him. "Why would you ask that?"

"I read your book while I was gone."

"You did?"

"I thought it might help me…" He shrugged. "I don't know, maybe get into your head. Figure things out."

She laid her head back down on his shoulder, feeling touched deep down to her soul. He cared enough about her to read her book. To try to figure her out. "I was pretty open about the verbal abuse. The constant criticism. But I never said anything about being physically abused."

"No, you didn't." He reached up to play with her hair, curling and uncurling a lock around his finger. "I was reading between the lines."

"What difference does it make?"

He tucked a finger under her chin, lifted her face to his. She'd never seen him look so serious. So sincere. "It makes a difference to me."

As embarrassing as it was, as much as she hated to admit to anyone that she had been that weak, she couldn't lie to him. "It only happened once."

"Once is too much."

"I know that. And the really sad thing is, to this day, I'm not completely convinced it wasn't my fault. Slightly hypocritical coming from me, huh?"

"Dare I ask how it could possibly be your fault?"

"We'd been trying to get pregnant for two years,

or so he thought. He finally insisted we go to a fertility specialist, and I finally had to admit that I'd been on the pill. That all the time he had been trying, I had been trying not to. So he hauled off and popped me one." She reached up and pressed her fingers to her left cheek.

Up until then Kirk had had her thoroughly convinced there was something wrong with her. That as a woman she should want a family. Should enjoy cooking and cleaning and changing dirty diapers. The fact that she didn't, or didn't right then, made her defective somehow.

But that day, when she felt the sting of his palm on her face, the explosion of pain in her eye, he had crossed some invisible line she hadn't even realized was there.

"This is going to sound strange, but in a way I actually felt relieved that he did it. I finally had an excuse to leave. To break free."

"If you weren't happy, why did you need an excuse?"

"So I wouldn't disappoint my parents. Because according to my whole family, I should have been happy with Kirk. I thought something was wrong with me. It never occurred to me that I just didn't love him."

"What happened after he hit you?"

"He bawled like a baby and begged me to forgive him. But at that point, I was a woman on a mission. I had my escape route and damned if I wasn't going to take it. I packed a bag and headed to my parents' house. For the first time in my life I felt free.

"By the time I got to their house Kirk had already called them and told them what happened. I expected them to be outraged at what he'd done."

"How could they not be?"

"Because apparently it was *my* fault. I had driven him to it."

They were so disappointed in her. So ashamed. They insisted that she go home to her husband, where she belonged, and beg *his* forgiveness. What she had done to him was cruel.

Maybe what she'd done was wrong, but they were her parents. They should have been on her side no matter what.

It was the moment she realized she was truly alone. And the only person in the world that she could rely on was herself. It was the day all her illusions about love and marriage and even family had been crushed to dust and swept away.

"I would never raise a hand to you." Zack touched her cheek, brushed her hair back from her face. "Not for any reason."

It was such a sweet gesture, the words so sincere, she got a little choked up. "I know you wouldn't."

He leaned forward and kissed her. One of those sweet, brushing-of-the-lips numbers. Soft, like a caress. And so damned tender.

Oh, man. If he kept that up she *was* going to cry.

So she kissed him instead. Really kissed him. And just as she began to get into it, into him, to sink into the warm swell of arousal, the damned phone began to ring.

Chapter Thirteen

"Ignore it," Zack told Miranda when she started to pull away. "If it's important they'll leave a message.

He kissed her lips, her chin, the curve of her neck. He couldn't get enough of her. The tastes and the scents. Just as it had been that night in the hotel, only different. Better somehow. More familiar maybe.

On his belt, his cell phone started to ring.

"Maybe you should answer it."

He eased her shirt collar aside and nipped her shoulder, felt her shudder in his arms. "You don't want me to do that."

He started unbuttoning her shirt, and she made a low, throaty sound. "You're right, I don't."

The only thing his reptilian brain could process was the need to get her naked, to sink himself deep inside of her again. He wondered absently if she had ever made love on a desktop before. But the instant his cell stopped ringing the desk phone started up again. "Oh, for cryin' out loud."

A wrinkle of concern set between her brows. "Maybe you should answer it."

Maybe she was right. Apparently someone was pretty desperate to get a hold of him. He looked over at the caller ID. It was his publicist.

This had damn well better be good.

Zack mumbled a curse and snatched the phone up. "What?"

"Turn on CNN."

"What?"

"Turn it on right now."

He called for this? "I'm nowhere near a TV, not to mention that I'm a little busy right now."

"Then find one, dammit, you need to see this. I have another call. Turn on the TV and call me back."

He heard a click, then dead air. "What the hell is going on?"

Miranda looked downright frightened now. "What's wrong?"

"I have no idea." He eased her to her feet and pushed himself up from the chair. "But we're about to find out.

Miranda watched the television in stunned silence as Zack's brother Rich, pasty-faced and sallow, was led in handcuffs into the Maryland Police Headquarters by two uniformed officers. A throng of media closed in like vultures on a carcass. Cameras flashed and microphones were thrust in his face. Reporters begged for a statement. A comment. Anything.

"Is it true you were caught soliciting the services of a prostitute?" one asked.

"Was she really only fifteen?" another asked.

Morbid curiosity kept her glued to her spot on the couch. It was the tenth time they had rerun the segment and she was still having a tough time wrapping her mind around it. Accepting the fact that Zack's brother was caught up in a sex scandal.

It had to be a mistake. A man like Rich couldn't possibly be capable of something so depraved and sleazy. He and Taylor were the perfect couple. They loved each other.

What did I tell you? that little voice in the back of her mind said, *Men are never what they seem.*

No, if Rich was anything like Zack, this had to be a misunderstanding.

She leaned over to peer into the kitchen. Zack was still pacing, cell phone glued to his ear. He'd been in constant contact with his publicist, agent and attorney. In between calls to them he'd been trying, without luck, to reach Taylor. It seemed as though the second the news broke, she'd slipped underground. The press, her friends, even her family claimed to have no clue where she'd disappeared to. But under the circumstances, even if they did know, they may have been hesitant to tell Zack.

He wanted to know if she was okay, and though he hadn't said it, Miranda was guessing that he needed to know if she planned to stand by Rich. Rich's career, and Zack's reputation, hinged on her actions.

"Still no comment," Zack barked to whoever was on the phone this time.

She'd never heard him be anything but perfectly polite on the phone, no matter who he was talking to. He was even cordial to the telemarketers who never failed to call her on a daily basis. Right now his nerves were like a rubber band stretched to its absolute limit. One more twang and she feared he would snap.

"Until I talk to Rich, we release nothing more to the press." He snapped the phone shut and turned to her. "There is now a mob of reporters outside my apartment building in Chicago."

Swell. "At least they don't know where you really are."

"Yet." He tossed the phone down on the coffee table and dropped onto the couch beside her. He sighed and dropped his head back against the cushions, massaged his temples. "I can't believe this is happening."

"It has to be a mistake," she said, even though deep down in her gut she feared the worst.

Apparently, so did he. "If this is a mistake, where is Taylor? Why isn't she at his side defending him? Why isn't she answering her damned phone?"

She wished she had answers for him. Wished there was some way she could make this better. The trouble with caring about someone was having to watch them suffer, and living with the helpless feeling that there wasn't a damn thing she could do about it. "When will you get to talk to him?"

"According to his lawyer, he should make bail sometime this evening."

A banner declaring breaking news and a photo of Rich flashed onto the screen.

"Now what?" Zack grabbed the remote control and turned up the volume, catching the correspondent midsentence.

"—former intern for the congressman has come forward claiming she was paid hush money to keep a relationship between herself and Richard Jameson quiet. And reportedly, she isn't the only one. Representatives for the congressman were unavailable for comment." Zack's picture replaced the shot of Rich, and Miranda's heart sank.

"Sources confirm that his brother, relationship guru Zackary Jameson, for whom the congressman and his wife were spokespeople, is also declining to comment. We'll bring you more as information becomes available—"

Zack muted the volume. "They're coming out of the woodwork now."

This wasn't looking good. Not at all.

She opened her mouth to utter a few meaningless words of comfort, but his phone started ringing again. With a heavy sigh, he picked it up from the table and flipped it open. "Yeah." There was a pause. "Yes, I was watching." He pushed himself up off the couch, resumed his pattern of pacing. "No, I haven't spoken with him yet." There was another pause, then he snapped, "Yes, David, I understand the concept of damage control."

By eight that evening the news, both national and local, had run footage of the intern confessing at an impromptu news conference, teary-eyed and remorseful, that she had indeed participated in a sexual relationship with her former boss and mentor. And she had been paid hush money to not only hide the relationship, but the fact that she had been pregnant with his child. A pregnancy he had coerced her into terminating.

Considering the infertility problems Taylor and Rich had been having, that particular betrayal, if true, was going to cut deep.

Poor Taylor. To learn that paying off his pregnant mistress had drained the money they needed for the fertility treatments. Miranda couldn't imagine anything more heartbreaking. To make matters worse, beneath the girl's tears, Miranda could see a hint of glee, a shadow of dollar signs in her eyes. Is that what this was about? Book contracts and talk-show interviews?

Sadly, people would listen, because she was young and pretty, and looked good when she cried. Which made her nothing more than a mediocre actress.

Zack still hadn't heard from his brother, and learned from Rich's attorney that he was still being questioned and probably wouldn't be released until the morning. In addition to the near-constant footage loop of the police hauling Rich away in handcuffs, clips of Zack lecturing and promoting his books began to hit the airwaves. He'd finally caved a few hours earlier and released a statement to the press. Something to the effect of, he was disturbed by the allegations, but would withhold any judgment or further comment until a time when all the facts of the case came to light.

Almost immediately the press had begun to speculate if this would mark the end of Zack's reign as the authority on family values. Would he jeopardize his reputation and stand behind his brother or, like the congressman's wife who had yet to show her face, wash his hands of him? And at this point, did it even matter?

They interspersed the coverage with shots of Rich and Taylor's Maryland town house and Zack's apartment building in Chicago.

She and Zack sat all afternoon and into the evening, side by side on the couch, eyes glued to the television—when he wasn't on the phone—waiting for new information. The Thai food Miranda had ordered for dinner sat mostly untouched on the coffee table.

By eleven the press began to speculate about supposed rumors of the congressman's kinky and unconventional fetishes. At that point Zack snapped off the television. "I can't watch this anymore. Every time I think it can't get worse, that it can't get any sleazier, it does." He rubbed his eyes with the heels of his palms. "This sucks."

She felt so useless. "I wish there was something I could say or do."

He touched her cheek, tucked her hair back behind her ear. "Having you here with me is all I need."

That just may have been one of the sweetest things anyone had ever said to her. Her family sure had never seemed to appreciate her companionship. Their reaction to her presence was typically one of exasperation or impatience. How many times had she been accused of being spoiled and selfish? Incorrigible and difficult. And all because she didn't want to do things their way. Because she preferred to think for herself and not follow the grand plan they had conceived for her.

Zack wasn't like that. Besides, this was not the time to worry about herself. About her problems. Her life. This was about Zack, and she would be there for him, no matter what.

She smiled up at him and took his hand, weaving her fingers through his. She liked touching him, just being close. "How did I manage to find you? How did I get so lucky?"

"You might feel different when I'm unemployed and living in squalor. Not to mention shame."

"That's not going to happen. You'll figure this out."

"And if I don't? If I'm royally screwed?"

She rested her head on his shoulder and closed her eyes. "I would love you, anyway."

She waited for some sort of response. Any reaction to the fact that in a roundabout sort of way, she had just told him that she loved him. But the reaction, the words never came. He just sat there beside her, motionless. And there was tension. She could feel it in his body, in the air.

She tried to convince herself that it didn't mean anything. It was probably just too much to ingest all in one day. He was overwrought and upset and it wasn't the time for spilling her heart out all over him.

Even though, if someone told her they loved her, she would be happy about it. Especially if she'd been repeatedly asking that person to marry her.

But she didn't want him to say the words until he was one hundred percent sure. Her marriage had been based on dishonesty and half-truths. With Zack, it would be different.

That didn't make her feel any less lousy.

The shrill of his cell phone plucked Zack out of a dead sleep at eight-thirty the following morning. He vaulted out of bed, instantly awake. He never slept this late. Must be a self-defense mechanism.

As long as he was asleep, he didn't have to deal with the fact that his career, his *life,* was in shambles.

It took a second to process that the ring was coming from the bedroom floor, from the vicinity of the jeans he'd tossed there last night.

Miranda was curled into a ball and still sleeping soundly beside him. He didn't want to risk waking her, so he grabbed his pants and carried them into the hallway, shutting the door quietly behind him. When he dug the phone out and looked at the display, he recognized the number instantly.

Richard.

He flipped it open, and in lieu of hello, said, "Are you okay?"

"I've been better." He sounded tired and defeated. Thin and hollow. "I wasn't sure if you would even pick up the phone. I thought you would be furious."

He'd tried to be angry, but it just wouldn't adhere. Rich would always be his baby brother, the scared little boy Zack took care of when their parents were too self-absorbed to notice them. "You're family, and family stands by each other. No matter what." He stepped into his office, holding the phone between his cheek and shoulder as he tugged on his jeans. "I want you to know that whatever this costs, I'll take care of it. If you want to fight this—"

"I'm pleading out to a lesser charge."

"You confessed?"

"Technically, no. In exchange for an allocution I took an extra year of probation." He paused, then said, "And I'm resigning my seat."

Which was as good as a confession in the eyes of the public. Zack felt sick to his stomach. "Are you sure that's what you want?"

"I just want it to be over. Your reputation..."

Was probably already damaged beyond repair. "Let me worry about that."

"I'm sorry, Zack. I didn't mean for this to happen. I tried so hard to...I'm sorry I'm such a screw-up."

"We'll get through this," Zack assured him. "We're a team."

"Maybe it's genetic. Or environmental. Maybe it was inevitable."

Their father cheated, so his sons would, too?

Zack didn't believe that. He believed that everyone made choices. And who was he to pass judgment? Didn't he have a pregnant mistress sleeping in the next room? Even he couldn't live up to his own stringent standards.

That had been *his* choice, and he was prepared to deal with the consequences. His brother would have to do the same.

"I love Taylor. There was just something missing."

"You don't have to explain." Deep down, he had already known that. Despite the front Rich put on, Zack knew something was wrong.

"I've lost everything," Rich said, sounding miserable.

"You haven't lost me. We just have to pick up the pieces and move on."

"You'll get through this, Zack. You were always the strong one." He sounded so positive, so sure of himself, that Zack wanted to believe it was true.

So why did he get the feeling the other shoe was about to fall?

Chapter Fourteen

It fell.

Two days later. Only, it wasn't one shoe. One shoe he could handle. One shoe was manageable.

This was a damned closetful of shoes.

All of them on the feet of the reporters and cameramen camped outside Miranda's condo. The story broke late the night before. In addition to the constant shrill of his phone, hers had begun to ring off the hook, as well.

Miranda peered through the curtains out his bedroom window to the mob across the street. "At least they don't know about your condo, otherwise they would be over here, too."

"And unless we want them to find out, you're stuck here," Zack told her. At least until one of their neighbors made the connection. Until they figured out that the guy linked with Miranda that they were seeing on the news was actually living in their neighborhood.

She shook her head in amazement. "How did this happen?"

"Someone started digging. Or someone ratted us out."

She shot him a questioning look over her shoulder. "Taylor?"

"Could be."

"Hell hath no fury?"

"Could you blame her if she did? Maybe this was inevitable. After all, it is a family tradition."

She shot him a questioning look.

"Yes. My dad cheated on my mom. But unlike Rich, he didn't bother trying to hide it. And instead of dealing with it, she drank herself into a stupor every night. I never understood why she didn't just leave him. *He* was the one who walked away. The one who finally left."

"She probably thought he would change."

"They fought all the time. My mom would

scream at him and throw things. Sometimes it was so bad, so loud, the neighbors would call the police. You can't imagine how embarrassing that was." He looked up at her. "You're the only person I've ever told that to."

"I'm glad you did."

He leaned back on his elbows and gazed up at the ceiling, the dots of morning sunshine filtering through the curtains like a monotone kaleidoscope. "I was so damned arrogant. Did I really think we wouldn't get caught? That people wouldn't figure it out?"

She sat on the bed beside him and leaned back on her elbows, mirroring his stance. "You're a hopeless optimist."

"I'm a fool."

"Well, if it's any consolation, my career is in for a serious blow, too."

"I would think all this publicity would be good for your image."

"Maybe, but my image won't mean squat when the publisher finds out how busy I've been not writing that book I owe them." It felt good to say the words, she realized. To finally admit it out loud. It felt like a huge weight off her shoulders.

"You haven't written any of it?"

"Not one damned word. I don't have the slightest clue what to say. I don't even know where to begin."

"Just write what you believe in, what's in your heart."

"Maybe that's the problem. Maybe I'm not sure *what* I believe in anymore. I was wrong about so many things. I mean, look at my life. Look what a mess it's in. Who am I to give people advice on anything?"

"You know the law."

"Just what the world needs. Another boring, crusty book on divorce law." She let her head drop against his arm. Being close to him, barely touching, made her feel better. It made things seem a little less hopeless. "The publisher wants another instant *New York Times* bestseller. I don't think I can give them that. In fact, I know I can't."

"How did you write the first book?"

"I had Ivy. She took what I wrote and breathed life into it. The thought of doing it without her...I sit at my computer staring at the screen, at the blank document, and I get this ache in my stomach. This bundle of nerves that makes me feel sick inside."

"Miranda, do you even like writing?"

Good question. "The truth is, I don't. I find it to be excruciatingly painful."

"So don't do it."

He made it sound so simple. "That's a swell idea, but I have a contract to fulfill."

"You're a lawyer. You know that any contract can be broken."

He was right, of course. She knew he was. With everything else in her life, it was just one more thing she didn't want to deal with. "Maybe I'm just not ready to admit that I failed."

He shrugged, making her head bob against his sleeve. "No one is perfect."

She looked up at him. "Boy, we're a pair, aren't we?"

He leaned over, kissed her gently, rubbed the tip of his nose against hers. "I think so."

Her heart instantly melted. Still there was that little voice in the back of her mind. The pesky one asking, did he love her? And if he did, why didn't he just say it?

He just needed time. They both did. She had to stop being so selfish, thinking only of herself.

She was about to wrap her arms around his neck, draw him close and really kiss him, but her cell phone chose that moment to begin ringing again. She closed her eyes and groaned. She was ready to flush the damned thing down the toilet. Except she knew that eventually she would have to answer the half-dozen messages her agent had left. And her family.

Ugh.

She would have to call them, too. She would have to figure out a way to explain why, when she was married, she couldn't be bothered to have a child, but having one conceived in the heat of passion during a one-night stand was perfectly acceptable. That was a call she was not looking forward to. Which is why, when she saw her parents' number on the display, she let it go to voice mail. Again. Then she shut the damned thing off and tossed it off the bed.

"You know what we need to do," she said.

"What do we need to do?"

She looped her arms around his neck. "We need to do something to take our minds off of everything that's happening. You know, like a diversion."

He grinned, got that devilish look in his eye. "What did you have in mind?"

"I'm glad you asked." She shoved at his chest, rolling them both over so she was on top and straddling his hips. She smiled down at him, going to work on his belt buckle. "Hold still and I'll show you."

Chapter Fifteen

The following afternoon, Miranda finally gave in and called her agent.

"Where the hell have you been?" she shrieked when her secretary connected them. "I've called you a million times!"

"Sorry. I just needed a little time to regroup."

"Every talk show, newspaper and magazine wants a piece of this. You're a legend."

A legend? For having an affair and getting knocked up? "Isn't that a bit of an exaggeration?"

"Are you kidding? You're on fire! Miranda, you dethroned the relationship king. Do you realize what this will do for women's rights and feminism? This is huge!"

Suppose she didn't want that distinction? That responsibility. It was one thing to be independent and modern, but her actions didn't necessarily reflect that behavior. She didn't want to give anyone that impression.

Didn't want to be responsible for ruining the career of the man she loved. The father of her child.

How did she get herself into this mess?

"How is the proposal going?" her agent asked.

She didn't know what to say. Maybe she should just tell her the truth. Tell her she couldn't do it. That she didn't want to.

"You know what, it doesn't matter. Whatever you have, toss it."

"Toss it?"

"They want to play on this while it's hot. I talked to your editor this morning. She wants a tell-all autobiography of how you brought down the relationship guru."

"What?"

"And they want it yesterday."

Oh. My. God. They were asking her to hang him. And they were supplying rope.

She closed her eyes and cursed silently. There was absolutely no way she could do that to him.

Never in a million years. She didn't care what it would do for her reputation or her career. No career was worth ruining another.

Her agent's tone went from excited to wary. "Miranda, I cannot stress how important it is to your career to get this book written."

"No," she said.

"No, what?"

"I'm not a writer. Ivy was the voice behind the first book. The talent. Not me."

She laughed. Actually laughed. "Is that all? Believe me that isn't a problem. Autobiographers use ghostwriters all the time. It will mean less money for you of course, but this will be so big I doubt—"

"No."

"No, what? No ghostwriter?"

"No to all of it. I can't write the book."

"This is your career we're talking about."

Her writing career. One that lately had done nothing but make her feel confused and inept. As of this moment, that part of her life was officially over. She would go back to law. It was in her heart. Her blood.

"My answer is still no."

"I don't see the problem, Miranda. It's not like you're going to marry the guy."

Maybe not right now, but eventually. She loved

him. And he loved her, too, even if he couldn't say it. For most of her life, it seemed as though something was missing. Something she wanted desperately but couldn't identify. And no matter what she got, it was never enough. Never right. Maybe all this time she'd had it backward. Maybe the trick wasn't just getting what she wanted. It was wanting what she had.

And she wanted Zack.

"Yes," she told her agent. "I am."

If there had been a worst-case scenario for Zack concerning his relationship with Miranda versus his reputation as a family man, they had found it.

He went out on a limb, and with her consent, released a statement that yes, they were expecting a child, and while they weren't married and had no immediate plans to tie the knot, they were in an exclusive, monogamous relationship.

Either the news had come too late, or people just weren't willing to accept what could have been interpreted as a do-as-I-say-not-as-I-do, attitude. Every day brought news of a speaking arrangement that had been canceled. Another endorsement dropped.

With each call, each new bit of bad news, Miranda could see his level of anxiety rising, see him become more and more frustrated, and it broke her heart. Didn't people realize that Zack was one of the good guys? He truly believed what he taught, but he was human. He made mistakes like everyone else.

She didn't dare tell him about the book her publisher had asked her to write. She feared it would be the thing to push him over the edge. All he knew was that her writing days were officially over. The publisher was threatening legal action and, as warped as it was, she felt relieved. In fact, she was actually looking forward to it. She could be a lawyer again. She felt as though she was back where she belonged.

But as good as she felt, Zack felt equally lousy. Maybe he would have been better off if he had been honest from the start.

And one week from the day the story broke, the bottom dropped out.

"It looks as though I'm going to have a lot of free time on my hands," Zack announced from the kitchen doorway. Miranda was making them dinner. Though the mob outside of her condo had finally given up and dispersed, she still spent the majority of her time at his place. Especially when meals were concerned. Since he kept more food than she did.

For all intents and purposes, they were living together. They just hadn't made it official yet.

She could tell by the look on his face that it was bad. "More cancellations?"

"It has been suggested that it would be best if I remove myself from the public eye for a while. Go on sabbatical."

"Is that what you want?"

"I'm not sure what I want."

He sounded so defeated, so dejected, she want to cry. She crossed the room and put her arms around him, pressing her cheek to his chest, the swell of her belly bumping his. She was starting to show, and she could swear she felt a flutter of movement last night while she lay still in bed, unable to sleep. Listening to Zack pretending to sleep beside her. "You'll figure it out, Zack. Everything will be okay."

"Everyone keeps telling me that."

"It's true. I don't even know how I know it. I just do."

"Everything is so screwed up right now, I don't know where to start."

"Maybe you should start by deciding exactly what it is that's important. Is it about the money? The celebrity?"

"Of course not."

"Do you like seeing your picture on the book jackets? Your name in the newspaper? Is it the thrill of getting up in front of a packed auditorium?"

"No. I like…helping people."

"So help them."

"And if they don't want my help?"

"You make them listen. Trust me when I say, this is a quality you excel at. Be honest about the fact that you made a mistake. Let them know you're human. I'll bet most people will respect you for it."

"And the ones who don't?"

"Those people don't matter."

"You have to be enjoying this at least a little."

What? She looked up at his face, to see if he was serious. "*Enjoying* it?"

"It's like payback for the radio interview."

He said it with humor, as if it was a joke, but she had the feeling he wasn't joking. Did he really believe she would find satisfaction in watching his career crumble?

Did he really think she was so heartless?

She backed out of his arms. "That was a terrible thing to say."

"You're right." He sighed and dragged a hand through his hair. It was getting long, and his beard had filled back in. Not that the disguise was going to do them much good now. "I'm sorry. Come here."

He pulled her to him and wrapped her up in his arms. She pressed her cheek to his chest, felt tears burn the corners of her eyes.

Pesky hormones. They were turning her into a big wuss.

He stroked her hair, her back. "How did everything get so screwed up?"

"We are not in the minority, Zack. Everyone has their cross to bear. What makes you so special that it should be easier for us?"

"I'm the relationship guru. This is my business."

Not anymore, she thought. Now he was just plain Zack Jameson. As confused and screwed up as everyone else.

That was just a natural part of life. If they didn't make mistakes, what would they ever learn? He of all people should know that relationships take work. If love came easy, without a fight, they might begin to take it for granted. She didn't want that to ever happen to them.

She rubbed her cheek against the soft cotton of his T-shirt. "I love you, Zack."

There was a pause, an almost imperceptible shift in his demeanor. Would he return the sentiment this time? Did he love her, too?

Finally he said, "But not enough to marry me."

He couldn't have been more wrong. But it was no longer about how much she cared for him. The real question was, how did he feel about her?

He was the most honest man she knew, until it came to talking about his feelings. It was as if he'd erected a wall between them, and nothing she did or said would knock it down. She understood that he'd had it rough. That he'd probably gone through life feeling inadequate and unloved. That his work as a psychologist was a way to somehow reconcile his past.

She got that.

And she knew that deep down he loved her, even if he couldn't say the words. But she refused to spend the rest of her life playing guessing games, being held at arm's length. She wanted more this time. She wanted it all, and she deserved it.

She stepped back from him and he dropped his arms to his sides. "How much I love you isn't the issue."

"What is the issue?" he asked, though she was convinced he already knew. And she refused to beg for it, to try to win his love. His affection. She'd played that game. Played and lost.

"The issue is why you want to marry me."

"You know why."

"Refresh my memory."

Now he looked angry. "What do you want from me, Miranda?"

Don't do this, she wanted to beg. Don't ruin it. "I only want to hear the words, Zack. I want to hear you say it with my own ears."

"What is this? Another test? You won't be happy

until you've stripped me of the last of my dignity? I moved across the country for you, risked my reputation. I've done everything humanly possible to prove my intentions. Sacrificed everything. And what have I gotten in return?"

Was he keeping score? For every good deed he expected an equal response?

She felt sick. Sick all the way down to her soul. Loving her shouldn't have been a sacrifice.

"I think I'm beginning to understand how your husband felt."

She felt every last bit of blood drain from her face, and something cold and black pierced her heart. If he was trying to sink low, to hit below the belt, he'd succeeded. "You want to take a swing at me, Zack? Would that make you feel better? Make you feel like a man?"

"You know I'm not like that."

She thought she knew him. Turns out she'd been wrong. He was a stranger.

"I don't want to hurt you, Miranda, but I can't be with someone who isn't willing to meet me halfway."

Was that an ultimatum? She married him or it was over?

She felt cold. So very cold. Maybe he really didn't love her after all. "I guess that's it, then."

"I guess so."

She could feel the tears building behind her eyes, welling up into her throat to choke her. She didn't want him to see her that way.

Trembling from the inside out, she walked to the door. She turned the knob and stepped out onto the porch into the blazing afternoon heat.

And he let her go.

He was an idiot.

And though it may have taken him a week to admit it to himself, he'd pretty much known all along. He knew when he'd made the choice to move here so he could convince her to marry him. It was an insult to her intelligence.

It's a wonder she hadn't tossed him out on his ear that first day.

And who the hell was he to lecture her about sacrifice? She had opened up her life to him. Her heart. She'd let him inside. What had he done? What had he really given her that she needed?

He was such an idiot.

The tough part now was telling her the truth and making her believe him.

He checked his reflection in the entryway mirror as he walked to the door. He was clean shaven, and the baseball cap had been officially retired. He was through hiding, pretending to be something he wasn't. He was prepared to face whatever life threw his way. Even if that meant dodging a few bullets now and then. The only important thing, all that really mattered, was that he and Miranda were meant to be together.

He grabbed his keys from the table and stepped outside, and the sweltering heat hit him like a wall of fire. Across the street, Miranda was stepping out her own door. Today was her ultrasound appointment and he planned to go with her.

She paused when she saw him. She was really beginning to look pregnant. Her belly peeked out from under the bottom edge of her T-shirt. He started down the driveway as she darted for her car.

Looks like she was going to try to outrun him. But this time he wasn't giving up so easily.

Miranda climbed into her car, the cloying heat scorching the insides of her lungs. With trembling hands she fumbled the key into the ignition and turned. As soon as the engine started she lowered all the windows and sucked in a breath.

If Zack's intention was to join her for her appointment, it wasn't going to happen. She wasn't ready to face him, to face the fact that it had been so easy for him to toss her aside, and she felt as though someone had reached into her chest and ripped her heart in two.

God, she was pathetic.

She was hopelessly in love with a man who, as far as she could tell, wasn't even capable of loving her back.

She stepped on the gas and backed into the street, jammed the car into gear, ready to floor it.

But Zack was there. He had planted himself in the street, right in front of her car.

Damn him!

"We need to talk," he said.

"I don't have time."

"We can talk on the way to your appointment."

"Not this time. I'm going alone."

"The deal was, we were going through this together."

But things had changed. With her foot on the brake, she gunned the engine. "Move, Zack."

He didn't budge from his spot. "Either I'm going with you, or we sit here all day like this. Your choice."

What did he want to do, throw a few more ultimatums her way? Bargain with her? Remind her again how spoiled she was? No, thank you. Hadn't he done enough?

"Don't think I won't run you down," she warned. At that very second she felt angry enough to do it.

And anger she could handle. Anger was good. She could wrap her hands around it and squeeze. It was the deep, heart-wrenching pain that was becoming too much to take.

He leaned forward and planted his hands on the hood. She could only imagine how hot it felt after sitting out in the sun all afternoon. "You'll have to run me over, then."

There was one major problem with living on a cul-de-sac. There was only one way out.

And he was in it.

"I'll do it," she warned, inching the car forward.

He sat on the hood. Actually sat down and made himself comfortable on the hood of her car. "Then you're taking me with you."

Fine. If that was the way he wanted to do it. If he wanted to ruin this special day. Fine. "Get in."

He narrowed his eyes at her. "You promise not to take off the second I get down."

She could. Hell, she should, but she was going to be an adult. After everything that had happened in the past few weeks, running down the father of her child would only confirm her neighbors' suspicions that she was completely certifiable. And get her a potential guest spot on Jerry Springer.

She jammed it into Park. "I promise I won't take off."

He slid off the hood, keeping his body close to the car as he walked around the passenger's side, opened the door and vaulted himself in. She waited until he was buckled in, then eased the car to the corner.

She couldn't help but notice that he wasn't wearing his disguise. He was clean shaven and looked as though he'd had his hair cut. And he did smell good. Even with the windows open his scent seemed to wrap all around her. Putting on the air-conditioning would only make it worse.

"I'm an idiot," he said.

Well, that's one thing they definitely agreed on. She searched the memory banks for something snarky to snap back at him, but nothing came to mind. Despite everything, she couldn't be mean. Couldn't hurt him. He was an idiot, but he couldn't help it.

"I want to be with you," he said. "I want us to be a family."

She'd heard that line before. But there had to be a catch. There was always a catch. "You know how I feel about that."

"I do. I knew exactly what you needed from me, but I was too much of an idiot to do it. To admit to you what you probably already knew."

Her hands had begun to shake again and she

gripped the wheel tighter. Tears welled up, making the road swim in front of her eyes.

"I love you, Miranda."

She sucked in a breath, a sort of half hiccup, half sob.

She was not going to cry. She was going to hold it together. "You sure you're not saying that just to get in my pants?" She joked.

From the corner of her eye, she saw him smile.

"I don't know if it means anything, but I've never said that to anyone before. Not a woman, not my parents. Not even Rich."

Suddenly the road was a total blur. She had to pull off to the shoulder to keep from killing them both. She rolled to a stop on the dirt shoulder and put the gear in Park.

"I may have felt it a time or two, but I never had the guts to say the words. To put myself out there." He took one of her hands, wrapped it up in his own. "Still love me? Or am I too late?"

He couldn't tell? She swiped away the tear that spilled over onto her cheek. "Duh."

He grinned and squeezed her hand. "Just wanted to be sure."

"And for the record. I did love you enough to marry you. If you'd have only asked the right way."

His eyes never straying from her own, he lifted

her hand to his mouth and kissed it. "Miranda, I love you, and I want to spend the rest of my life with you. Will you marry me?"

She didn't know if she should laugh or cry. So she did both.

And she said yes.

"Would you like to know the sex?" the technician asked as she smeared goo on Miranda's belly.

Miranda looked up at Zack. He stood beside the table holding her hand. They never had made a decision. She had been for, Zack had been against.

"You want to know?" he asked her, and she nodded. He smiled and told the technician, "We want to know."

Miranda anxiously watched the screen as the first images of their baby appeared. It just looked like a confusing jumble to her, but the technician seemed to recognize what she was seeing. She ran the probe across her belly and back again, typing on the keyboard with the opposite hand. "Can you tell if it's a boy or girl?"

She shook her head. "They don't seem to want to cooperate."

She looked at Zack, then they both looked at the technician and said in unison, *"They?"*

"The doctor never mentioned multiples?"

"Never," Miranda said, feeling shell-shocked.

Zack's expression mirrored her own. "Wouldn't we have heard two heartbeats?"

"With maternal twins it's not uncommon for the hearts to beat together."

"Maternal, as in identical?" Miranda asked.

And Zack asked, "Are you sure?"

She pointed to the fuzzy image on the screen. "Here's one spine, here's the second."

Miranda squinted at the screen, and sure enough, she could see them. Twins.

Twice the diapers and the crying and the feeding. Twice the work, and more sleepless nights.

And twice the love. And she was sure Zack had plenty to go around.

The babies never did cooperate and reveal their gender. Already showing their father's stubborn streak, she figured. But they did get a screen shot that very clearly showed them both.

"Your doctor will talk with you at your next appointment, but everything looks great," the technician assured them. "Congratulations."

After she left, Miranda sat up and wiped off the rest of the goo.

"Twins," Zack said, shaking his head, as though he still couldn't quite grasp the concept.

"When you knock a girl up, you really knock her

up," she joked, and he flashed her a wry grin. "Are you totally freaked out?"

"Not totally." He looked down at the ultra-sound image. "I think I might even be getting used to the idea."

She pulled her shirt down over her belly, her twins, and swung her legs over the side of the table. "We have so many plans to make and things to buy."

"I'd like you to do something for me," he said. "I want you to call your parents and try to patch things up."

She opened her mouth to object, to give him sob stories and excuses, then closed it again when she saw the look on his face. It was lined deep with regret and sadness.

"Despite everything that happened, they're still your parents. Your family. They won't be around forever. If you don't at least try to work it out, you'll regret it when they're gone." He reached up and brushed a wisp of hair back from her face. "Trust me on this one."

She did trust him. "I'll call them tonight."

"If you want them to accept you for who you are, that means accepting them for who they are, too."

He was shrinking her again, but she let it slide this time, since his words made a lot of sense. And they were coming from his heart.

"Besides." He placed a hand over her belly. "They're going to be the only grandparents these guys have."

"Not to mention that my parents notoriously love to babysit. And we're probably going to need a breather now and then."

His hand felt warm on her tummy. Warm and safe. She knew that Zack would never hurt her.

"If it wasn't for these two, we may never have reconnected," he said. "We would be living totally different lives."

And she couldn't imagine spending her life with anyone else. "Does that mean we have to spoil them?"

"Maybe a little." He grinned down at her, brushed her hair back from her cheek and tucked it behind her ear. "You know, for years I searched for the perfect woman. The perfect mate."

"And?"

"And I got someone even better." He brushed his nose against hers, smiled that sexy smile. "I got you."

* * * * *

Welcome to cowboy country...

Turn the page for a sneak preview of
TEXAS BABY
by
Kathleen O'Brien
An exciting new title from
Harlequin Superromance for everyone
who loves stories about the West.

Harlequin Superromance—
Where life and love weave together in
emotional and unforgettable ways.

CHAPTER ONE

CHASE TRANSFERRED his gaze to the road and identified a foreign spot on the horizon. A car. Almost half a mile away, where the straight, tree-lined drive met the public road. He could tell it was coming too fast, but judging the speed of a vehicle moving straight toward you was tricky.

It wasn't until it was about two hundred yards away that he realized the driver must be drunk…or crazy. Or both.

The guy was going maybe sixty. On a private drive, out here in ranch country, where kids or horses or tractors or stupid chickens might come darting out any minute, that was criminal. Chase straightened from his comfortable slouch and waved his hands.

"Slow down, you fool," he called out. He took the porch steps quickly and began walking fast down the driveway.

The car veered oddly, from one lane to another,

then up onto the slight rise of the thick green spring grass. It just barely missed the fence.

"Slow down, damn it!"

He couldn't see the driver, and he didn't recognize this automobile. It was small and old, and couldn't have cost much even when it was new. It was probably white, but now it needed either a wash or a new paint job or both.

"Damn it, what's wrong with you?"

At the last minute, he had to jump away, because the idiot behind the wheel clearly wasn't going to turn to avoid a collision. He couldn't believe it. The car kept coming, finally slowing a little, but it was too late.

Still going about thirty miles an hour, it slammed into the large, white-brick pillar that marked the front boundaries of the house. The pillar wasn't going to give an inch, so the car had to. The front end folded up like a paper fan.

It seemed to take forever for the car to settle, as if the trauma happened in slow motion, reverberating from the front to the back of the car in ripples of destruction. The front windshield suddenly seemed to ice over with lethal bits of glassy frost. Then the side windows exploded.

The front driver's door wrenched open, as if the car wanted to expel its contents. Metal buckled hideously. Small pieces, like hubcaps and mirrors, skipped and ricocheted insanely across the oyster-shell driveway.

Finally, everything was still. Into the silence, a plume of steam shot up like a geyser, smelling of rust and heat. Its snakelike hiss almost smothered the low, agonized moan of the driver.

Chase's anger had disappeared. He didn't feel anything but a dull sense of disbelief. Things like this didn't happen in real life. Not in his life. Maybe the sun had actually put him to sleep….

But he was already kneeling beside the car. The driver was a woman. The frosty glass-ice of the windshield was dotted with small flecks of blood. She must have hit it with her head, because just below her hairline a red liquid was seeping out. He touched it. He tried to wipe it away before it reached her eyebrow, though, of course that made no sense at all. Her eyes were shut.

Was she conscious? Did he dare move her? Her dress was covered in glass, and the metal of the car was sticking out lethally in all the wrong places.

Then he remembered, with an intense relief, that every good medical man in the county was here, just behind the house, drinking his champagne. He found his phone and paged Trent.

The woman moaned again.

Alive, then. Thank God for that.

He saw Trent coming toward him, starting out at a lope, but quickly switching to a full run.

"Get Dr. Marchant," Chase called. "Don't bother with 911."

Trent didn't take long to assess the situation. A fraction of a second, and he began pulling out his cell phone and running toward the house.

The yelling seemed to have roused the woman. She opened her eyes. They were blue and clouded with pain and confusion.

"Chase," she said.

His breath stalled. His head pulled back. "What?"

Her only answer was another moan, and he wondered if he had imagined the word. He reached around her and put his arm behind her shoulders. She was tiny. Probably petite by nature, but surely way too thin. He could feel her shoulder blades pushing against her skin, as fragile as the wishbone in a turkey.

She seemed to have passed out, so he put his other arm under her knees and lifted her out. He tried to avoid the jagged metal, but her skirt caught on a piece and the tearing sound seemed to wake her again.

"No," she said. "Please."

"I'm just trying to help," he said. "It's going to be all right."

She seemed profoundly distressed. She wriggled in his arms, and she was so weak, like a broken bird. It made him feel too big and brutish. And intrusive. As if touching her this way, his bare hands against the warm skin behind her knees, were somehow a transgression.

He wished he could be more delicate. But he smelled gasoline, and he knew it wasn't safe to leave her here.

Finally he heard the sound of voices, as guests began to run around the side of the house, alerted by Trent. Dr. Marchant was at the front, racing toward them as if he were forty instead of seventy. Susannah was right behind him, her green dress floating around her trim legs.

"Please," the woman in his arms murmured again. She looked at him, the expression in her blue eyes lost and bewildered. He wondered if she might be on drugs. Hitting her head on the windshield might account for this unfocused, glazed look, but it couldn't explain the crazy driving.

"Please, put me down. Susannah... The wedding..."

Chase's arms tightened instinctively, and he

froze in his tracks. She whimpered, and he realized he might be hurting her. "Say that again?"

"The wedding. I have to stop it."

* * * * *

Be sure to look for TEXAS BABY,
available September 11, 2007,
as well as other fantastic Superromance titles
available in September.

HARLEQUIN *Super Romance*

Welcome to Cowboy Country...

TEXAS BABY

by Kathleen O'Brien

#1441

Chase Clayton doesn't know what to think.
A beautiful stranger has just crashed his
engagement party, demanding that he not
marry because she's pregnant with his baby.
But the kicker is—he's never seen her before.

Look for TEXAS BABY and other fantastic
Superromance titles on sale September 2007.

Available wherever books are sold.

HARLEQUIN *Super Romance*

**Where life and love weave together
in emotional and unforgettable ways.**

ATHENA FORCE

Heart-pounding romance and thrilling adventure.

Professional negotiator Lindsey Novak is faced with her biggest challenge—to buy back Teal Arnett, a young woman with unique powers. In the process Lindsey uncovers a devastating plot that involves scientists from around the globe, and all of them lead to one woman who is bent on destroying Athena Academy...at any cost.

LOOK FOR

THE GOOD THIEF

by Judith Leon

Available September wherever you buy books.

AF38973

The latest novel in The Lakeshore Chronicles
by *New York Times* bestselling author

SUSAN WIGGS

From the award-winning author of *Summer at Willow Lake*
comes an unforgettable story of a woman's emotional journey
from the heartache of the past to hope for the future.

With her daughter grown and flown, Nina Romano is ready to
embark on a new adventure. She's waited a long time for dating,
travel and chasing dreams. But just as she's beginning to enjoy
being on her own, she finds herself falling for Greg Bellamy,
owner of the charming Inn at Willow Lake and a single father
with two kids of her own.

DOCKSIDE

"The perfect summer read." —Debbie Macomber

*Available the first week of August 2007
wherever paperbacks are sold!*

MIRA®

www.MIRABooks.com   MSW2475

REQUEST YOUR FREE BOOKS!

2 FREE NOVELS PLUS 2 FREE GIFTS!

 Silhouette®

SPECIAL EDITION®

Life, Love and Family!

YES! Please send me 2 FREE Silhouette Special Edition® novels and my 2 FREE gifts. After receiving them, if I don't wish to receive any more books, I can return the shipping statement marked "cancel." If I don't cancel, I will receive 6 brand-new novels every month and be billed just $4.24 per book in the U.S., or $4.99 per book in Canada, plus 25¢ shipping and handling per book and applicable taxes, if any*. That's a savings of at least 15% off the cover price! I understand that accepting the 2 free books and gifts places me under no obligation to buy anything. I can always return a shipment and cancel at any time. Even if I never buy another book from Silhouette, the two free books and gifts are mine to keep forever.

235 SDN EEYU   335 SDN EEY6

Name	(PLEASE PRINT)
Address	Apt.
City	State/Prov.	Zip/Postal Code

Signature (if under 18, a parent or guardian must sign)

Mail to the **Silhouette Reader Service™:**
IN U.S.A.: P.O. Box 1867, Buffalo, NY 14240-1867
IN CANADA: P.O. Box 609, Fort Erie, Ontario L2A 5X3

Not valid to current Silhouette Special Edition subscribers.

Want to try two free books from another line?
Call 1-800-873-8635 or visit www.morefreebooks.com.

* Terms and prices subject to change without notice. NY residents add applicable sales tax. Canadian residents will be charged applicable provincial taxes and GST. This offer is limited to one order per household. All orders subject to approval. Credit or debit balances in a customer's account(s) may be offset by any other outstanding balance owed by or to the customer. Please allow 4 to 6 weeks for delivery.

Your Privacy: Silhouette is committed to protecting your privacy. Our Privacy Policy is available online at www.eHarlequin.com or upon request from the Reader Service. From time to time we make our lists of customers available to reputable firms who may have a product or service of interest to you. If you would prefer we not share your name and address, please check here. ☐

SSE07